# CHAS WILLIAMSON

*Sweetheart Romances of Paradise: Book Six*

# HOMECOMING

*in Paradise*

Print ISBN:   978-1-64649-187-2

eBook ISBN: 978-1-64649-188-9

Year of the Book
135 Glen Avenue
Glen Rock, PA 17327

# *Dedication*

## *To Janet*

*Homecoming in Paradise* is a story about returning home after a long journey.

I think about all the journeys I've taken. Some, like college, were long and tedious. Others, like work trips, were shorter and wearisome. But the thing that's made a difference is the homecoming, because you were waiting.

My life really began when we married—so young and in love. We had little more than that. Remember how we used a box for a table for the first three months because we couldn't afford furniture? Yet, my heart would rejoice when I came home to you. I was convinced then (and still am) that I was the richest man in the world because I had you to share my life with.

Our journey together has mostly been magical—oh, there were the occasional down times and bumps in the road... but coming home to you always made it better. There are no words I can write that could truly state how I feel about you. The word *love* is just the beginning, and what we have is so much more precious.

There's no denying God made us for each other. At some point, our journey may separate us for a brief while, but rest assured, that final homecoming will eclipse any memory we've already made. Imagine, together forever, with a love sweeter and deeper than even those first, dewy-eyed days when we started.

God has blessed me richly and the best blessing... is you. And I'm glad it was you. Out of all the people He created through eternity, He chose you for me... and me for you.

And so, this book is dedicated to you, the woman who holds my heart in the palm of her hand. And I love it. I love you, forever, and will love you even more a million years from now. Thank you for growing old with me.

*I asked God for a friend... and He sent you.*

*I begged Him for a soulmate... and He sent you.*

*I prayed for true love... and He sent you.*

*I dreamed of heaven... and He sent you.*

*Then I thanked Him for my blessings... because He sent you.*

*True love lasts forever!*

# Acknowledgments

To God, for blessing me so richly, and not only in material things. Because of Your love and blessings, my heart is filled with wonderful memories of love and happiness. Thank You for guiding me to choose the higher road and not succumb to hate, bitterness and a life of disappointment that awaited me.

To my best friend, just for being you. Realize this— you have helped me become the man I am today. And the life we've created is one I'm so proud of. (P.S. To me, you are perfect.)

To Demi, editor, publisher and book whisperer extraordinaire, for helping me become a real author.

To my beta readers, Janet, Sarah, Connie, Mary, and Becca for your suggestions, help and tweaks to make my stories of love and hope even better.

To the men and women who have sailed the seven seas in the service of this great nation. I am fully aware that it was the sacrifices of veterans of all services that have allowed me to live a life of peace and comfort. And given me the freedom to write my silly tales of love. Ron, Scott and Dad, I'm proud and thankful for all you've done. *Go Navy!*

To Travis and those who have encouraged me, even when it was fashionable to do just the opposite, I hope I can pass on encouragement to others like you've done for me.

# The Families of Paradise

## The Lapp Clan

Aubrey Lapp – Connor's wife
Connor Lapp – Aubrey's husband
Isaac "Devo" Golden – Aubrey's step-brother
Leslie (Lapp) Golden – Connor's sister

*Family Friends*
Didi Phillips-Zinn – Luke Zinn's wife
Hannah Espenshade – owner of Hannah's Bakery, Sam's wife
Luke Zinn – Didi's husband
LBJ Zinn – son of Didi and Luke Zinn
Rachel (Domitar) Landis – friend of the family
Rebecca Stoltzfus – Amish neighbor
Sam Espenshade – Hannah's husband

## The Rohrer Clan

Daisy Elliot – Joe's close friend and co-worker
Jake Elliot – Daisy's husband
Joseph Rohrer, MD

## The Campbell Clan

Ashley Campbell – Harry's wife
Ben Miller – Sophie's husband
Darcy Campbell – mother of Edmund, Harry, Henry, and Margaret Campbell
Edmund Campbell – Henry's brother, Tara's husband
Ellie Campbell – Henry's wife
Harry Campbell – Henry's brother, Ashley's husband

Henry Campbell – co-owner of Campbell Farms, Ellie's husband

Maggie May Campbell – eldest daughter of Henry and Ellie

Margaret Campbell – co-owner of Campbell Farms, Henry's only sister

Sophie Miller – owner of the Tea Room, Henry & Ellie's best friend, Ben's wife

Tara Campbell – Edmund's wife

## *Prelude*

*December*

Margaret Campbell waited in the queue to exit the cruise ship. *By myself.* She was thankful she had splurged for the private stateroom, because her three companions only seemed to be interested in partying and hooking up with strangers. She assumed, when none of them had shown for breakfast, that's where they were. Despite plans to meet and explore the city, Margaret was alone. And that was fine with her. One-night stands? *Definitely not my style. Love is something deeper than sleeping with someone you don't know.*

Aldous Huxley was correct when he wrote, *"Oh Brave New World, which has such people in it."* After years of preparation, Margaret was ready to settle down and finally start living her life. A real life, close to her family, was waiting back in Paradise, Pennsylvania. And as soon as she finished her apprenticeship, she'd return home to be with the people she loved.

The little boy in front of her was swinging back and forth as his parents lifted him off the deck surface. The father looked down at him and smiled. "Are you ready to visit the sea lions?"

"Will they roar, Daddy?"

The man laughed. "We'll have to wait and see."

It was finally Margaret's turn at the departure kiosk. The young steward roved his eyes from head to toe, raised his eyebrows and smiled. "Heading ashore, Ms..." he took a second glance at her passport and keycard, "Campbell?"

"That I am."

"Are you doing anything special in Puerta Vallarta?"

"Not really. Perhaps some shopping."

The attendant handed the documents to her with a wink. "Just remember, if you take any transportation, only use the taxis you find here at the terminal. Have a great day, ma'am."

"And you as well." Margaret eased her way across the gangway, passed through the terminal and stepped onto the main drag of the town. One of her goals today was to pick up a souvenir for her niece and namesake, Maggie May Campbell, her brother Henry's eldest. At six, Maggie May was a fashionista and held a special place in Margaret's heart. The little girl's jet-black hair and brown eyes definitely matched those of her mother, Ellie. In fact, all four of Ellie's daughters resembled their mother as opposed to the green eyes and reddish-brown hair of their father, Margaret's brother, Henry.

A teenage girl bumped into Margaret despite plenty of room on the sidewalk. A quick check verified her purse was still securely slung over her shoulder. Margaret always practiced excellent situational awareness, a skill her brother Henry had taught her. A former Royal Marine Commando, Henry had schooled her about not only keeping an eye out for threats, but how to defend herself. And she'd put those skills to good use twice—once with a would-be mugger and the second time with an over-zealous date.

A quick glance over her shoulder revealed the same youth a few steps behind Margaret. When the girl gave a quick nod to someone ahead, the act raised Margaret's awareness. *Pickpockets.*

Margaret slipped into a small bar that was situated along the street. A waitress walked over to her. Without taking her eyes from her tracker, Margaret ordered. "Virgin Pina Colada, *por favor.*"

The woman responded, "*Si, senorita,*" and then walked off.

The young pickpocket was now pretending to examine some trinkets a street vendor had displayed. But Margaret was sharper than that. Her young stalker probably thought Margaret was an easy mark—a slight young woman alone in a strange city. *Mess with me, sister, and you'll be in for quite a surprise...*

Drawing her eyes from the girl, Margaret glanced around the rest of the pub. They skipped over, but quickly returned to a man occupying a barstool at the other side of the room. *Do I know you?* His face seemed very familiar. Was he someone she'd met when she attended Penn State or maybe over the last two years when she'd worked at a vineyard in Napa Valley? *No, that doesn't seem right.* But when he rubbed his chin, his identity came back to her. *Oh my God! It's him!*

In just a few seconds, she moved until she stood next to the man. He glanced in her direction, then did a double take. The man's eyes seemed to draw her in. Margaret's pulse was racing and she couldn't help but smile. "Hi, Joe. Do you remember me?"

\*\*\*

Joe Rohrer sat wallowing in self-pity. *Stinks to be me.* Earlier that morning, he'd turned down his sister's offer to accompany her and her husband on a tour of the city. And while Joe loved his parents, he had disembarked to get away from them and keep from losing his temper. If it wasn't his mother constantly bringing up his last girlfriend, Leslie, it was his father who kept pointing out the "available women" on the ship.

To maintain his sanity, Joe had come ashore to get a few hours of peace and quiet. As if one could call sitting in a bar along the main street where mariachi music was blaring, peace and quiet. The presence of someone to his left captured his attention. A gorgeous young lady with fair hair and a number of freckles covering her beautiful face leaned against the bar next to him. She stood out from the majority of other women he'd seen this morning. While it seemed the normal garb for this hot and humid day was skimpy swimsuits and sarongs, the stranger sported light brown shorts and a flowered top.

The smile that slowly covered her face had started in her green eyes. "Hi, Joe. Do you remember me?"

Okay, she did look familiar, but he couldn't place her. He turned to give the pretty woman his full attention. Though slight, he depicted an English accent. "I believe we might have met, but I'm not sure where or when."

She sipped her drink and then winked at him. "Are you sure? I thought I was more memorable than that."

*So gorgeous.* "I really wish I did. Enlighten me. How do I know you?" He took a taste of his drink.

"You dated my sister-in-law."

The liquid stuck in his throat, He had to force it down. *Does Leslie have another male sibling I don't know about?* "Are you a Lapp?"

She giggled. "Nope."

If it's not Leslie, it must be Aubrey. "Are you related to Aubrey?"

"Aubrey who?"

The glass in his hand was shaking, because his hand was trembling. "Stettinger, well, she's Aubrey Lapp, now."

The beauty shook her head and snorted. "Must be a fan of the movie *Witness*. Seems you have a thing for women named Lapp. Unfortunately, that's not my last name."

Now his mouth went dry. *Tara?* The man Tara married had a sister, with fair hair. The girl's identity suddenly came back to him. "Wait. You, you're Margaret Campbell, aren't you?"

CHAS WILLIAMSON

She extended her hand. "Look at that. You do remember me." A goofy grin covered her face as she gazed at him.

Those green eyes seemed to glimmer. Joe remembered his manners. "Please sit down."

"I was beginning to wonder if you would ever ask. Are you here on vacation?"

He nodded back in the direction of the ship terminal. "Here on a cruise. What brings you into this bar?"

Her giggle was like sunshine on a rainy day. Margaret pointed to a young girl outside. "Avoiding the pickpockets." She turned her attention back to Joe. "I wanted to do a little shopping, and see some of the city. Want to come with me?"

For the first time since he'd left Pennsylvania, a warmth started in his chest. Joe finished his drink and stood. "I thought *you'd* never ask."

\*\*\*

The twin scents of grilled meat and coconut sunscreen were just icing on the cake of a nice afternoon. The tall man by her side obviously wasn't into shopping, but really seemed to enjoy Margaret's company. From the corner of her eye, she caught his smile as he watched her. "What's so funny, Joe?"

He took a swig of bottled water. "You are, Margaret Campbell. A vineyard? I don't know that I've ever known a woman who wanted to own a vineyard."

Margaret picked up a brightly painted ceramic piece. "Out of all the things we've talked about, you focus on the wine?"

Joe shook his head. "No, not that. Your drive, your vision. And what are you going to name it?"

"The Scottish Lass Vineyard."

"So cool. Never would have guessed the little town of Paradise would become so international. First the Italian tea room, and now a Scottish winery. What could be next, a Mexican restaurant?"

The alarm from her phone interrupted the conversation. "Oh, my goodness. Look at the time. I've got less than an hour to be back on board the ship. We should head back to the dock."

A frown made an entrance on the man's face. "I don't want the afternoon to end."

"Well, I don't want to miss the boat and be stuck in this tourist town. What time do you need to be back?"

After glancing at his watch, he replied. "Three hours."

She offered her hand. "Then we should say goodbye. I enjoyed this afternoon. Maybe when I move back to Lancaster, we could continue this?"

He quickly shook his head. *Can't wait that long.* "I'll come back with you." He searched the street and then took her hand. "Let's take a cab." The gentleman opened the door for her and she scooted across the seat. He spoke to the driver. "*Habla anglaise?*"

The driver shook his head. "*Habla espagnole, no anglaise.*"

Joe's brows furrowed as he cast a questioning look at her. Margaret smiled and replied. "Cruise ship terminal, *si?*"

The driver nodded. "Ah, *si*. Cruise ship." The driver pulled out into the crowded street and headed toward the docks.

Margaret picked up on the sad expression on her friend's face. "What's wrong?"

A deep sigh. "Today's been lovely. I hate to see it end. When are you moving back to Lancaster?"

"A couple of months. I'm still learning, you know?"

"I can't comprehend why you would leave the lovely Napa Valley to return to Pennsylvania."

She patted his hand. "I miss my family. There's..." She stopped. The driver had turned out of traffic onto a side street.

Joe studied her reaction. "Everything okay?"

Chills ran down her spine. "The ship terminals were on that road. Where's he taking us?" The driver's eyes fell on them in the mirror before quickly looking away. She raised her voice and pointed to her left. "Cruise ship terminals, *por favor*."

Margaret caught his smirk as he nodded and pointed up the hill. "Cruise ships, *si*."

She whipped around to face Joe. "Take off your belt, now."

He laughed. "Whoa. That's a little forward."

"We're about to be robbed, or worse. Hand it to me. *Now*."

"Robbed?"

She could wait no longer. Her fingers found the buckle and she opened the clasp. With a forceful yank, the leather strap was now in her hands. A glance in the mirror found the driver's eyes wide as he watched her. The cab was accelerating as it climbed the hill. As loud as she could, she commanded the driver. "Cruise ship terminals, now!"

The man simply smiled and pointed in front of them. "Cruise ship, *si*."

In a move that would have made her brother proud, Margaret whipped the belt over the driver's head until it was at his neck and then she pulled back harshly. To gain leverage, Margaret shoved her knee against the back of the seat. The cab veered to the right as she tightened the binding. The car slalomed to a halt in front of a telephone pole. The man struggled against the restraint.

Margaret's voice was fierce. "Where were you taking us?" She released the hold, just a little so he could speak.

"This is my shortcut."

Joe yelled, "I thought you couldn't speak English."

The driver was gasping for breath. "This are the only words I know."

Margaret yanked harder.

"The docks are downhill. Why were you taking us up the hill?" She viciously cinched the belt against his throat.

The man held up his hands, as if he were surrendering. She relaxed the grip. "Okay, okay. I get paid twenty U.S. dollars for every tourist I take into the mountains. *Lo siento*, I mean, sorry. Nothing personal."

Margaret's voice was cold and calculated. "Neither is this. Hand me your phone and the car keys." When he hesitated, Margaret increased the pressure. The man turned off the car, held up the keys and a cell phone. Joe grabbed them. "Your things will be in the trunk. Sweet dreams." She pulled the belt tighter. The driver struggled, and then lost consciousness.

Joe's mouth fell open. He whispered, "You killed him."

"No, he's just out cold, but not for long. We need to get out of here. Throw those things in the back, close the lid and let's get moving."

Margaret opened the door. A crowd was starting to assemble, many voices rising as they took in the scene. She quickly returned Joe's belt and then removed her sandals. Rohrer's mouth was hanging open as he stared at her.

Margaret nodded in the rough direction of the docks. "We don't want to get detained by the Federales. It was nice seeing you again, but I hope you can run fast. Right now, it's every man, and woman, for themselves. Thanks for a wonderful afternoon." She kissed his cheek quickly. "Hopefully I'll see you again someday in Paradise." Without another word she dashed off down the hill.

# Chapter One

*May*

*T*he hearty scent of fried bacon lured Margaret from her sleep. She was tired, partly because her body was still on West Coast time, but also because the homecoming party her family had thrown lasted until early morning.

After a quick shower, she descended the stairs to take in the pandemonium. The seven little princesses sitting around the table were in various stages of eating (and wearing) breakfast. Four of the children belonged to her brother Henry while the remaining three could claim her other brother, Edmund, as their father. All of the girls were singing, just not the same song. Dolls and stuffed animals littered the table. The noise and activity were mind-boggling.

"Morning." Her pregnant sister-in-law Ellie's tired smile greeted her as Margaret swung open the kitchen door. "Don't you look happy this morning? Bet you're glad to finally be home in Lancaster. Welcome back to Paradise."

"It's paradise being surrounded by family." She'd missed everyone, but especially Ellie. The bond between the two women was strong and deep. Warm memories of their first meeting filled her heart. Back then, her family had lived in rural Scotland. During Ellie's initial visit with Margaret's family, Margaret had witnessed first-hand the ability Ellie and Henry had to share emotions and sometimes thoughts. Hard to believe, but when Henry introduced Ellie to her, Margaret knew she'd just met the woman whom her brother would marry. Less than six months later, he did.

Margaret's first trip to America had been to visit Ellie. But a short eight weeks after that happy time, Ellie disappeared and was declared dead. Henry refused to believe the police. For days seemingly without end, Henry and Margaret had searched Oahu for Ellie and finally discovered the location where she was being detained. Together, the siblings had rescued Ellie. The violent liberation had almost cost Henry his life, but now the pair had been married for almost ten years.

"Here you go, Maggot." Maggot had been her father's nickname for her. Margaret turned to her mum, Darcy. The aromatic trace of peach hovered around the hot cup of tea Darcy sat before her. "So good to have my wee lass home again." Darcy crushed Margaret in her arms.

Margaret had to wait until her mother relaxed her grip before answering. "So good to be where my heart has always been."

"Well, look who's gracing us with her presence—sleeping beauty. About time you rolled out of bed." Her brother Henry walked over to brush his lips against her forehead. "We've got a lot to do today."

Darcy slid a heaping plate of bacon, sausage, potatoes and eggs in front of Margaret. "Let your sister eat in peace. The poor thing's nothing but skin and bones. Need to fatten her up if you ask me. Of course, you'll probably work her to death."

Henry laughed. "Come on, Mum. Most of the heavy lifting's already been done." Her brother's eyes engaged hers. "While some people were tanning themselves in the California sunshine, others have been working hard to make *her* dreams come true." Henry was talking about her winemaking endeavor. She had designed the operation, but the construction had happened while Margaret was on the West Coast. She couldn't wait to see how the venture was progressing.

Margaret sipped her peach tea. "I've been the silent partner for too long. Can't wait to put everything I learned in college to work. There's lots of changes I want to make."

Henry tousled her hair. "Wondered when you'd get tired of us spending your money." The family fortunes had come in the way of a windfall when they rescued Ellie. Margaret and Henry had also freed another girl who'd been a hostage, not knowing her father was the richest man in Hawaii. The man had been so grateful to get his daughter back that he'd awarded both siblings a considerable reward. Henry and Margaret had merged a great deal of their fortunes and founded Campbell Farms.

"It's not that you haven't done well, but I think I can increase our yields and efficiency."

Ellie shot her a smile. "I'm excited about you starting the winery. What are you going to name it, Campbell Wines?"

Margaret shook her head. "I did consider that one, but I like the name 'The Scottish Lass' better. What do you think?"

Ellie's brown eyes twinkled. "That has a certain ring to it."

Henry laughed. "I think a better name would be the 'Prodigal Sister'." Margaret turned to face her brother. He touched her cheek. "I, for one, am glad you came home."

The door flew open and Edmund, the youngest of her brothers, waltzed in. He made the rounds of the princesses at the table, kissing and teasing his daughters and nieces until they were exceptionally wound up.

Darcy stormed in from the kitchen, wooden spoon in hand and red covering her face. "Edmund! I'll have none of this. You get them all excited and then leave me with my hands full. Be gone."

The mischievous expression on the young man's face couldn't be missed. He turned to Margaret and winked. "I think it would be a good time to make our exit now."

\*\*\*

"I'm impressed with the crop diversity and all that's been accomplished."

Henry touched her arm. "Last year was the first we've turned a profit." He didn't need to explain how the family had spent the last several years building the infrastructure. This was all part of the plan

Henry, Ellie and Margaret had written out on a napkin in the hospital where Henry was recovering from the life-threatening injuries he'd suffered the night they'd freed Ellie from captivity.

The longer they drove, the more Margaret's excitement grew. Only one segment of the complex remained for inspection. The hour-long tour of the farm and operations had exceeded her expectations. Fields were planted with summer crops. A grove of evergreen trees was neatly trimmed in expectation of holiday sales. More than a dozen large hothouses were stuffed to capacity. Auxiliary buildings and sheds were neatly organized. Nutrient-rich effluent from the fish hatchery was used to feed the plants growing in the glass houses. But the most exciting sight had been the rows and rows of grapevines maturing in what once had been a pasture filled with beef cattle. Vines she had planted three years ago, before moving to the West Coast. Almost thirty acres worth.

Edmund turned into the gravel lot and dropped the transmission into park. Margaret's chest swelled with pride as she took her first look at the large oak building. This was it, the arena she'd designed that would house the Scottish Lass endeavor.

Margaret swallowed hard. "Just like I dreamed, only prettier." She opened the truck's front door and waited until Henry climbed from the rear seat. "I can't believe this." Henry gently pinched her arm. "Ouch!" She turned to face her eldest brother. "What was that for?"

15

Henry wrinkled his nose when he smiled. "Wanted you to know this isn't a vision. This is real—your dreams and wishes, come to life."

Edmund offered his arm. "Let's start upstairs in the receiving bay."

The three siblings climbed the small bank to the top floor of the barn. The woody scent of the exposed oaken timbers filled the air. Equipment, fermenting tanks, fruit presses and storage silos occupied the upper floor. She strolled around the apparatus just as a curator would amble through her museum. Everything was shiny, new and waiting to be used.

Margaret took one last deep breath before descending the stairs to the ground floor which housed the catacomb, where hundreds of barrels would one day age the wine she'd make. The titles for the flavors she'd create, such as Scottish Knights, Maiden's Dew, Heather in the Moonlight, Dark Side of the Vine and Sweet Wee Lass bounced around in her head. It was dark down there, and so exciting to be in this place where Margaret would make her mark on the world.

A whirring noise caught her attention. Henry motioned with his head. "Come along. I'll introduce you to our mechanic and handyman."

The rough-hewn boards were coarse and uneven when she touched the door to close it. A man sporting a tank top stood braced against the bottling machine as he attached a bracket. His bulging muscles didn't even pretend to hide the United States Marine Corps tattoo on his right arm. He wore some purple ball cap, which he quickly pulled from his head when he noticed her.

His smile appeared genuine as he extended his hand. "You must be Margaret. I've heard so much about you, I feel like I know you. It's really a pleasure to finally meet you. I'm Isaac, Isaac Golden."

*So cute.* His hand was warm and firm. "I'm Margaret Campbell and the pleasure is all mine. My brothers told me you've been the overseer of this project."

"Just the equipment stuff. Your brothers deserve the credit for how well the building turned out. During the construction, I think they lived here." His eyes bored into her soul. "May I ask a personal question, ma'am?"

"Uh, sure." She could guess his question was either going to be funny or embarrassing by the way her brothers tried to hide their chuckles.

"These two," he pointed at Edmund and Henry, "refer to this place as Maggot's Lair. When I asked what that means, they told me I'd have to wait and ask you in person. And my curiosity has gotten the better of me. What did they mean?" She felt her cheeks heat. Isaac's hands went up in front of himself. "Oh, no. They set me up, didn't they? Sorry, Ms. Campbell. I didn't mean to offend you."

Edmund was chortling, emitting a sound like a ball bouncing down the road. Henry's reaction was less concealed. Apparently, her brother couldn't help himself. The man was doubled over with laughter.

She gave them a look that she hoped was nasty. "The first word happens to be my Pop's nickname for me, and the Scottish meaning of lair is a burial plot. So, Mr. Golden, according to my brothers, you are standing in my grave."

\*\*\*

"Here you go, doc." Jake Elliot handed over a bottle of hard apple cider before plopping down in the lawn chair. "Sorry it didn't work out. Daisy was just trying to be helpful."

Joe Rohrer took a deep breath. "I know. Your wife has a heart of gold. I believe we all know the reason the lady left so quickly." His friends had set up tonight's blind date. And tonight's girl was not only drop dead gorgeous, she was smart and funny. But once again, Joe had doomed any potential relationship. His track record with women was pathetic. He had fallen in love three times, but for whatever reason, the ladies he loved always chose someone else.

Daisy returned from the driveway. She had walked his date, the research scientist, out to her car. Long before Jake had even warmed up the grill. His friend now stood before him and reached for his hand.

*I'm such an idiot.* "Let me guess, I was too intense, right?"

The lady's smile was sad. "Just a tad."

Jake reached over to hand his wife a bottle. "I think asking her to name every man she'd ever dated might have been okay... until you asked her to give odds on which ones she'd choose over you."

Daisy took a swig of her drink. "Either that or when you asked if she would ever consider you as a possible husband."

Joe knew the answer, but the question begged to be asked. "Too soon?"

Those blue eyes sparkled as she shook her head. "Do you even remember her name?"

"Uh, Melody?"

"Nope. It was Melanie."

Joe rubbed his fingers through his hair. "I hate dating. I dislike the games. I loathe being alone. Why can't I just find a woman who wants me for me, the first time she sees me?"

Daisy answered, "Good things take time. The Bible tells us the wise man built his house on solid rock, not shifting sand. And I'm pretty sure the same applies to relationships. I'm sorry, but people don't come wearing signs that say, 'I'm the one you're supposed to be with,' or 'Pick me'. It will take time, but Joe, I believe deep down inside of me that God has someone special planned for you."

"I hope you're right, because obviously I'm incapable of finding someone on my own."

Jake patted his shoulder as he walked to the grill. "Acknowledging you have a problem is the first sign on the road to solving that issue."

*What?* "Why would you even say something like that?"

The man turned to him. "Because Daisy's right. I believe the Almighty designed us with the perfect person He wants us to be with. And no matter what we do, when the time is right, He'll make it happen." Joe caught a momentary glimpse of pain in Jake's eyes as he stared at Daisy. "Just listen to your heart... and don't wait as long as I did to realize what was right before me."

Joe watched Daisy run into her husband's outstretched arms. Daisy had waited eighteen years for Jake to realize he loved her. The words were but a whisper as he watched his friends embrace. "Have mercy, Lord. Please don't make me wait that long." Perhaps it was an evening breeze, but it felt like someone ruffled his hair.

## Chapter Two

*June*

*T*he mouth-watering scent of fried zucchini lingered in the air. It was Wednesday night and the entire family, all fifteen of them, were gathered around the table.

Margaret wiped her mouth with a napkin. "Mum, that was great. Can't tell you the last time I've had breaded squash sandwiches for supper."

Darcy smiled and then replied, "There's more in the kitchen, but don't forget, I made fresh apple crisp for dessert, compliments of your sister-in-law Ashley's recipe. Save room for that. I'll dish it out. Be right back."

Tara, Edmund's wife, chimed in, "The girls and I made homemade strawberry ice cream for tonight. I'll give Mum a hand by dipping out some on top of the apple crisp."

Margaret's mouth was watering. "You don't have a clue how much I've missed our family meals, and the delicacies served at this very table."

Edmund took a sip of his iced tea as he leaned back in the chair. "Huh. Well, I can't wait for our sweet corn to mature. The ears we've been getting from South Carolina just don't have the same flavor as what we grow on this land."

Henry, now the patriarch of the family, simply smiled as he glanced around the table. "It really doesn't matter what wonderful food Mum makes to feed us, it's the people around the table that make this a truly blessed time."

The adults in the room replied in unison, "Amen."

Harry, Margaret's third brother, stood. "All this talk about desserts is making me hungry."

"What? You had four sandwiches, two baked potatoes and three helpings of brussels sprouts," Harry's wife Ashley admonished. "How can you still be hungry?"

Margaret had to stifle a giggle. While Harry was in no way overweight, he was a large man. Ashley, on the other hand, was petite in every way, except her loving heart.

Harry kissed his wife before teasing back. "Since you eat less than a bird, I need to make sure I eat our fair share."

Darcy and Tara strolled through the door. They both carried trays filled with the delicious-looking treats. Her mother was all smiles. *Mum is in her glory, feeding all of us and having her grandchildren with her.* All girls. Maybe this time Ellie would have the son that Henry wanted. This evening was the first time in a long while that Margaret's heart felt full.

Harry placed his empty dish on the table and then glanced at his mother. "That was tasty. Is there more?"

Darcy's grin covered her face. Margaret recalled that when people asked for seconds, her mother took it as a compliment. "Help yourself, son." The older woman nodded in Margaret's direction. "Bring some for your sister. She needs to build up her stamina for all the hard work she's going to be doing."

Quick to shake her head, Margaret replied, "I'm good for right now and besides, I want to save room for s'mores later tonight."

Henry gazed at her with a question in his eyes. "S'mores? Where are you getting s'mores? I want some."

"Why, here. Aren't we having a bonfire tonight? We used to have them twice a week."

Henry's expression was sad. "We're all so busy that we kind of got away from having them. You know, kids and all. But maybe we can plan one, if you want."

*Life's changed that much?* "You're too busy for family time?"

Ellie touched her arm and answered softly, "Our evenings are filled with bath time and stories."

Henry was now standing next to her. "It's a new chapter in our lives, Maggot. It's the days of unicorns, princesses and fairy tales. You're more than welcome to join us, if you'd like."

She turned to Edmund. "Is it the same for you and Tara?"

His smile was melancholy. "It is a magical time in life."

Harry walked back into the room, his plate filled with a second helping of apple crisp. For years, the bond between Harry and Margaret had been strong and close. "What about you and Ashley? Want to have a bonfire with me?"

Harry briefly glanced at his wife before giving his full attention to Margaret. "We were going to work on our marketing plan tonight. New book launch next month, you know?"

The earlier warmth in her chest had begun to turn to a chill. Margaret shifted until she faced Darcy. Before she could speak, her mother shook her head. "Don't look at me. Wednesday night is bridge night. Sorry about that."

Margaret stood and picked up her plate, preparing to take it into the kitchen. "You shouldn't be sorry, Mum. I'm the one who should be remorseful."

All eyes were on her. Henry asked the question that seemed to be on everyone's face. "What do you mean?"

"I guess while I was out building my future, the world I loved slipped through my fingers. Good night, all."

***

Jake placed three bottles on the table. Joe met his friend's eyes. "Why three?"

"I don't think one's going to be enough."

Joe leaned his head back to stare at the ceiling. "I overcompensated, didn't I?"

Jake scratched his scalp. "We'll let Daisy analyze the play-by-play, but to be honest, Joe, you barely said two words to your date."

Daisy returned from the front door. She took in the number of brown hard cider bottles in front of Joe. "Ah, maybe that explains it. Were you buzzed?"

"Come on, Daisy. You know me better than that. Why would you even ask?"

The smile that usually graced Daisy's face had been replaced by a big frown. "It was like you ignored Georgia. Treated her as if she didn't exist. When she left, she asked me what she did to offend you. Didn't you like her, or what was the problem?"

"No, I did like her. She was smart and nice and very cute..."

"But what?"

"Can I be honest with you?"

Jake laughed. "This oughta be good."

Daisy whipped around to her husband. "Stop it. Don't make fun of Joe. You know, just because you have someone doesn't give you the right—"

Her husband held his hands up in front of his chest. "Daisy, you are absolutely correct." Jake moved to face Joe. "I'm sorry. I meant no harm. I'm going to walk into the rec room to give you two some peace and quiet."

Daisy was silent until her husband disappeared. "What happened tonight?"

Joe shook his head. "She just wasn't the one."

"I don't understand."

"This will make no sense, I'm sure. When I do find the right girl, I'll know. I've been in love three times in my life and I can tell you the exact moment

I realized it in each case. Okay, maybe it wasn't the first time I met them, but there was an attraction."

"And you didn't feel anything with Georgia?"

"To be honest, she made me feel tired."

"Tired? What's that mean?"

He ran his hand through his hair. "It just felt like having a relationship with her was going to take a whole lot of effort."

"Of course. You don't just meet someone and everything is perfect from that second forward. Even the happiest of relationships requires effort... and lots of it. Nothing is free. You have to work without rest to get something good in return."

"Look, I don't expect you to understand, but after the inevitable happens, I just can't see putting in the effort for her."

Daisy sat across from him. "The inevitable?"

"Yes. When she inevitably decides there's someone else she wants more than me. I just don't think the desire to try and change her mind is greater than the energy I'm willing to expend."

"Not every girl is going to want someone else."

"So you say, but let's consider my history. Tara married Edmund. Aubrey ended up with Connor. And Leslie fell for Isaac. I'm in a rut. The same thing will happen with the next girl, mark my words."

"Okay, Dr. Rohrer, if you say so. I remember something about this from my psychology class. What did they call it?" Daisy placed her hand against her cheek and looked away. "Oh yeah. The self-fulfilling prophecy."

"What?"

She stuck her finger in his face. "Keep telling yourself every relationship will fail, and you know what? They will. You need to be more positive."

"Maybe we should just put this on hold for a while."

"You mean trying to set you up on dates?"

"Yes. Let's give it a break."

Daisy nodded. "I think that's a great idea. Let's let it happen naturally and who knows? Maybe the woman you'll someday marry will suddenly show up when you least expect it." Daisy took a swig of her drink and motioned with her head. "Why don't you come watch some television with Jake and I? We'll even let you pick out the show."

"Okay. I'll be in shortly." Joe knew Daisy was only trying to help, but honestly? Meeting a woman on his own that would really want him? *Like that will ever happen.*

***

"The Scottish Lass? How cool! I think there's a lot we can do with that theme."

Margaret was watching the woman's eyes. As an excellent judge of people, Margaret could tell Leslie loved what she did, and that happened to be interior design. The two women were standing in the bare storefront that would one day house her shop. "Really? Tell me what you've got in mind."

Leslie's eyes changed and seemed to focus on something in the distance. A smile filled her face. "In the center of the back wall should be your coat of arms, with Scotland's flag bracketing it on either side. Random pieces of stone artwork, like the Celtic infinity knot or even a Celtic cross would help set the mood. Accent it with old-time photos, perhaps of a wedding where the groomsmen are wearing kilts. Directly out front, I think we should have a garden lined with a cobblestone walk, moss growing in between the stones. Perhaps replicas of those famous horseheads, uh, I forget what they're called..."

Margaret was being drawn into the vision as she watched the woman's excitement grow. "Are you talking about Kelpies?"

Leslie's blue eyes seemed to glow. "Yes, yes. That's it. Keeping the open beams and adding grids to the store windows to provide a Tudor-like appearance might be nice. And we need a rustic fireplace right next to the tasting bench. For the barstools, we'll cloak them with tartan fabric. Perhaps an artificially aged painting of you, walking in the highlands in a long white dress with a darkening sky, and the logo of your winery in the corner of the painting."

Leslie stopped and wrapped her arms around herself. It seemed Margaret was almost lost in the daydream of it. "To enhance the atmosphere, perhaps a suit of chainmail, or, ooh, ooh, ooh, I know. I read one time about a castle in Scotland that had stone carvings of fairytale creatures. If we had some of those mounted on a shelf in the corner..."

Margaret laughed and shook her head. "That castle's in Wales. I'm Scottish, not Welsh."

"I'm sorry. It's kind of hard to plan for something you've only ever read about, but not yet experienced. I was telling Isaac I really want to visit the United Kingdom before we have children. In fact—" A ringtone sounded from Leslie's pocket. "Excuse me for a second, that's my emergency cell. Do you mind?"

"No, go ahead."

Leslie smiled. "Thanks." The other woman pivoted away. "Hello? Hi, Aubrey. What's wrong?"

*Aubrey?* The name was unique. *Where have I heard that name before?*

"I'd be glad to pick up the prescription. Anything else you need? Saturday? Oh, don't worry about it. I'll see if I can find someone else. No, I mean it. Just concentrate on taking care of Cooper. I'll finish up here and stop by the drug store. See you within the hour. Bye-bye." Leslie smiled. "Sorry about that. I need to get going."

Margaret's curiosity was getting the better of her. "Who was that?"

"My brother Connor's wife. Aubrey."

"That's a pretty name. So her last name is... Lapp?"

Leslie stared at her strangely. "Um-hmm. Why do you ask?"

"That name is strangely familiar. Maybe I met her when I used to live here."

Leslie shifted her weight. "No. Aubrey moved here from New York City about three years ago, right after the accident."

"Accident?"

"A truck hit her and broke both her legs. My house is wheelchair accessible. That's why she moved here."

"I see."

Leslie checked her watch. "I really need to go. My nephew's ill and I need to pick up some medicine for him. Sorry to end our visit so abruptly. May I contact you next week to finish?"

"Sure. Is there anything I can do to help?"

"No." Leslie stared at her briefly. "Maybe. Ever played golf?"

"A couple of times, at Penn State. Why?"

"We have a foursome on Saturday mornings. With Cooper being sick, Aubrey had to back out for this week. Would you like to take her place?"

*Hmm. A chance to make new friends.* "Sure, why not."

Leslie's smile was wide. "Great. It'll be a lot of fun. How about I text you later with the details?"

Margaret knew she was smiling. "I like that idea. Oh, by the way, what was your sister-in-law's maiden name?"

"Stettinger. Why do you ask?"

"Just curious. See you Saturday."

"Okay. See you later."

Margaret watched her new friend drive off in her Suburban. *Stettinger, Stettinger. Why does that name sound so familiar?* Almost an hour later, the memory appeared in her mind. And along with it, the face of the man she'd left standing on the street in Puerto Vallarta.

## *Chapter Three*

*Later That Week...*

"I think I'm going to pass on the ball game tonight." Joe removed the sweat-soaked Barnstormers cap and wiped his forehead with an equally wet arm. "You and Jake should just enjoy your time together. I appreciate that the two of you are looking out for me, but I'll be fine."

*I'm sweating like a pig. I better drink some water.* "I've got plenty to do... I'm planting flowers and mulching the beds... Yes, Daisy. I promise not to overdo it... yep, planning on taking lots of breaks... and I guarantee I'll stay well hydrated. Give my best to Jake. See ya."

Daisy was a great friend, but lately she seemed to be overly protective. For example, Chelsea, one of the new nurses, had befriended him. Joe liked the new girl, but when Daisy saw what was happening, she had a long talk with Joe. And it was good that she reminded him how office romances rarely succeeded, and gave some fitting examples of the consequences.

A low-flying plane passed overhead, probably from the airport in Smoketown. Joe shook his head. *How well I remember...* He was referring to his failed romance with Tara. They had both been medical providers, initially at the same, but then later, at different practices. When Tara left Joe to go back to her former boyfriend, it had almost ruined him. For the first time in his career, he seriously considered leaving Lancaster.

"Ouch." Joe smacked at a gigantic horse fly that had taken a bite of his forearm, but he missed. Walking into the basement, he grabbed a bottle of water. After draining the container and dropping it in the recyclables, he headed back outside to his chores.

Opening up the door to the old Chevy pickup took him back in time. The truck belonged to his dad, one of the few remnants from the farm days. Joe had learned to drive in this old beast. No power steering, no power brakes, and a "three on the tree" gear shift on the steering column were reminders of the simple life. He'd had his first kiss in this truck, with a Mennonite girl named Grace... Grace what? Joe couldn't remember her last name, but did recall the sweetness of her lips. She'd tasted like the peach she'd eaten.

He smacked the side of his face to break the train of his thoughts. "Won't be getting any kisses today." Joe took a quick glance at his reflection in the driver's mirror. "Or probably anytime soon."

*That was what Daisy would call negative thinking.* Drawing a deep breath, he re-engaged his own eyes. *Daisy would tell me to think positive.*

*Here goes.* "Joseph, you handsome man, you... Could today be the day when the woman of your dreams suddenly appears? You know she will!" He couldn't help himself. Joe laughed. "Yeah, right. Like *that's* going to happen."

\*\*\*

Margaret opened the rear hatch of her Land Rover and lifted the pink and white golf bag from the back. The scent of fresh-cut grass filled the air. Occasional white puffy clouds dotted the azure blue sky. As she closed the trunk, she heard someone call her name. Turning, she quickly found the owner of the voice—Leslie Golden.

"Morning, Margaret. So glad you could join us. Why don't you drop your clubs in the cart and join us for the pre-game cup of coffee? We still have a few minutes before our tee time."

Leslie's kindness made Margaret feel welcomed. She followed her friend to a table in the clubhouse. Two other women were sipping drinks. Margaret immediately recognized the petite blonde.

"Hey ladies, this is Margaret Campbell. And Margaret, this is the rest of the foursome, Rachel Landis and Didi Zinn." Rachel had curly brown hair which framed a very happy looking face.

Margaret extended her hand. "Nice to meet you, Rachel." She turned to the pretty girl, whose blue eyes smiled at her as she shook hands with Margaret. "And I do believe I've seen you before. You're the morning news anchor from the Harrisburg station, aren't you?"

Didi waited to reply until after the waitress took Margaret's drink order. "Yes, I'm Didi Phillips-Zinn. Glad you could join us this morning. Rachel told me you're starting a winery in Paradise. How's that going?"

"I'm still getting things in order. The last piece of equipment arrived this week. And maybe she didn't say anything, but I just hired Leslie to design the store."

Didi smiled. "That's so cool. Maybe we could do a news piece on... what's the name of your business?"

Leslie quickly answered for her. "The Scottish Lass." Margaret took in her friend's expression. Leslie was beaming. "The building is beautiful and so well organized. The décor of the sampling room and store will put the final touches on it, but the heart of the story should be Margaret's vision and drive. That's the real tale to be told."

Rachel giggled. "What Leslie isn't telling you, Didi, is that she has a vested interest in this business. Devo works there."

*Devo?*

"Wasn't that a rock band in the '80s?"

Rachel again laughed. "Yes, but that's not why Leslie's husband got his nickname."

The waitress returned with Margaret's iced coffee.

"Okay..."

Rachel made her voice sound deep. "It's because he's devoted to God, family and the Corps, in that order."

Margaret was confused when all three of the other women raised their fists and replied in unison, "Ooh-rah!"

Rachel continued, obviously teasing Leslie. "Of course, since they got married, Leslie may have changed his order of devotion. In case you haven't picked up on it yet, she loves to be the center of attention."

Leslie patted her lips with a napkin, but when she removed it, a devilish smile shone through. "I'm not the drama teacher, Rachel, you are. And besides, since Rachel and Kim got married, it's rare for her to come out of the house. You know, Devo and I were wondering, what do you two do all the time? Read over scripts? Inquiring minds do want to know."

Didi giggled and then smiled at Margaret. "They think the reason I came was to play golf, but it's more for the comic relief." Didi glanced at her watch. "Okay ladies, time to work our way to the cart."

When they arrived at the tee, Leslie encouraged Margaret to lead off. Her drive was straight but short, making it only a third of the way to the green. Leslie and Rachel had much better success. Didi's efforts were similar to Margaret's and the two found themselves spending time together on the first six holes.

Didi's ball was in the rough, about ten yards from Margaret's effort. "I forgot about this part."

Margaret eyed her strangely. "This part of the course?"

"No, the part where I'm not as talented as those two. And not as competitive, either."

"It looks like you and I are much the same. I play for the company and exercise, not really for the love of the game and especially not for winning." She hesitated. "So, what's it like to be a television star?"

"It's just a job, much like everyone else has."

"Really? I think it would be fun."

Didi swung, sending her ball to the center of the fairway. "There was a time when everyday was exciting and a joy to be alive." The blonde pursed her lips together as she waited for Margaret to take her shot.

Margaret's ball didn't end up where she intended, but instead was now in a sand trap.

Margaret glanced at Didi. The girl dabbed at her eyes with a tissue. "Everything okay?"

Didi nodded, but her face didn't support her expression.

"Are you sure?"

Didi pocketed the tissue and then rubbed sanitizer on her hands. "Sorry about that. I remember Luke and it makes me sad sometimes."

They slowly walked out of the rough. "Is Luke your ex?"

"No. Luke is my husband. When I started at the station, he was my cameraman. Life was wonderful, sharing it with him. The best time of my life."

"Oh, I'm sorry. Are you divorced or separated?"

They stopped so Didi could take her swing. The ball plopped onto the green. The woman's eyes seemed to stare at the ball. "He's missing in action. Luke didn't return from the war when his unit came home."

*Oh my God!* "I'm so sorry. I didn't mean to pry. It has to be so difficult."

"He was in the reserves and received the call to report to duty on Christmas night." Didi laughed sadly and shook her head. "He comes from a family of Marines. His dad used to accuse him of being a coward for not signing up with the Corps. I was afraid he'd do something incredibly stupid, so I proposed to him, right there, that night. We were married the next morning and he left the following day. And much to my everlasting regret, he volunteered for hazardous duty and never made it back to the base. I haven't seen him since."

*How incredibly horrible.* Things were a little blurry for Margaret. She felt moisture on her cheeks. "I don't know what to say. Something like that would destroy me."

Didi handed her a clean tissue. "Don't be sad for me. I was lucky enough to be with him, even for a short while. God only gives you what you can handle. My parents moved here to support me. I've got lots of great friends. In fact, your brother visits with me frequently. He comforts me and instills hope that Luke is still alive... somewhere."

*Henry comforts her?* "I didn't know you knew Henry."

"My best friend used to work for him at Campbell Farms. Henry always tells me how the military is relentless in searching for MIAs. His words give me hope and I pass that optimism onto LBJ."

"Lyndon Baines Johnson?"

"Luke Bryan Junior, our son. We were only together for our wedding night and LBJ was the result."

"Wow, I'm astonished and at a loss for words. I'm sorry."

There was a little more strength in Didi's smile. "Don't be. Another good friend of mine is always saying there's a reason for everything. It's all a part of God's plan. I rest my faith in that belief and I know Luke is still alive."

Margaret touched her arm. "Then I believe he is, as well."

"Hey, slow pokes. Will you be joining us this week or should we come back next Saturday?" Leslie and Rachel had walked over. Leslie's voice had that teasing quality, until she glanced at Margaret. "Everything okay?" She was now directly in front of Margaret. "You look sad. Tell you what, you can take twenty strokes off your total today."

Margaret shook her head. "You'll still win."

Leslie laughed and the day seemed to suddenly get better. "You have me all wrong. For me it's the time with friends and not *just* about winning."

Rachel shook her head. "Pu-lease! Let me translate for you. In her vocabulary, that means, it's all about Leslie not losing."

Leslie shook her head and smiled. "Rachel and I were thinking about heading over to Essence of Tuscany for lunch. What do you girls think?"

Didi shrugged. "Sure. Why not? How about you, Margaret?"

It felt like she'd known these girls for years. *Such good friends.* It had been a long time since she'd felt included—anywhere. "That would be delightful."

\*\*\*

Joe was soaked with sweat. It had been years since he'd physically worked this hard. *Almost like being on the farm again.* But the flower beds were shaping up nicely. The pansies he'd planted this morning were lifting their faces to the sun. Gerber daisies, petunias, anemones, paint brushes and begonias now decorated his backyard. Joe had selected each flower yesterday from the garden store in Smoketown.

He stood and arched his back, practicing counter-balance stretching for his weary muscles. Perhaps Daisy was right. Taking up gardening as a hobby not only looked like it would be fun, but he already noticed a drop in his stress level. Joe anticipated holding get togethers in the backyard and hearing his guests marvel over the landscaping. Perhaps, after a shower, he'd go shopping for lawn ornaments to add some décor.

The water was cold as he guzzled down yet another bottle from his fridge, then threw away the container. A full pickup load of mulch was waiting for him. *Back to work.* He caught his reflection in the side-view mirror and the image took him back to when he was a teen, helping out on the farm. "Man, am I filthy." His hands and arms were dark from the mulch. There was a smear on his forehead from where he'd wiped away the sweat. "That shower's going to feel good."

He had barely turned his head when a crashing noise sounded behind him, followed by a sharp pain when something struck his back. He turned to discover the mirror was shattered. A quick search identified the culprit. There was an orphaned golf ball in the yard.

***

The round was progressing nicely, but Margaret's luck got even worse. She appeared to be chasing the ball everywhere, but Didi walked along to keep her company. Their conversation was natural and continuous.

After one drive took Margaret well off the fairway, Didi snickered. "I think I've figured you out."

Margaret eyed her strangely. "What do you mean?"

"The reason your shots take you out here is because you love the outdoors so much. Definitely not a city girl." Didi's smile warmed her. "I envy you... living with your family on a farm in the country. When I was a little girl back in South Dakota, my best friend's family had a ranch. I spent a lot of time there, riding horses. I wish I had a farm and a pony LBJ could ride."

Margaret couldn't help but smile. "Well, maybe history is repeating itself." She waited until Didi looked up, her eyes questioning Margaret. "It just so happens one of your friends *owns* a farm... and a couple of ponies for children to ride... and horses. You know, in case you ever want to come over by yourself."

Didi's mouth dropped open. "You own a farm? I thought you had a winery?"

"The majority of the land my brother manages belongs to me. The farm is over three hundred acres and there's lots of riding trails. I've got a Shetland pony named Sugar Foot who is very gentle. Why don't you bring your son over sometime?"

Didi's smile was ear to ear. "LBJ would love that. I'm really glad we met."

"I am, too." It seemed like the possibility of a true and real friendship just might happen between them.

On the sixteenth hole, it was Margaret's turn to tee off first. Leslie approached her, holding a golf club. "I see you're using a fairway wood. Try my driver. It's got excellent balance. I think you'll get more distance off the tee."

Margaret squinted at Leslie. "Really think that will help?"

"Maybe, why don't you see?"

*Anything would be an improvement.* "Okay. Thanks."

Margaret pushed the tee into the ground and topped the ball. Taking a step backwards, she took a few practice swings then stepped up to the tee. "Here goes nothing."

Margaret wound up and slammed the driver into the ball. Her eyes followed the flight. She got a lot more distance, but unfortunately her ball hooked far, far to the left, disappearing behind a hedge of holly.

"You were right, Leslie, but unfortunately, my ball ended up in someone's backyard."

Leslie's voice was high. "Uh, why don't you forget that ball and try it again?"

Margaret turned to Leslie. The other woman's eyes looked funny and she seemed to be blushing. "I'll go look for it. It's no problem."

"No, no." Leslie ripped a new ball from her bag and then presented it to Margaret. "Use this one. You can have it. Just forget about the other one."

The look on Leslie's face creeped Margaret out. "No, I'll just walk over there and get my ball." She caught the expression Leslie shot at Rachel. "I'll be right back."

Didi took a step toward her. "I'll help you look for it." The pair headed toward the house.

Margaret's voice was low and she nodded back at the other two women. "I get the distinct feeling Leslie doesn't want me to look for my shot. Or am I imagining things?"

"I picked up on that as well."

"Do you know why?"

Didi shook her head. "I don't have a clue." They were approaching the border. "I see a gate along the side of the hedge."

"I hope my errant shot didn't break any windows." Margaret opened the gate. An old green pickup truck was parked in the middle of the yard. Standing next to the driver's door was a man. He was holding a white object—Margaret's ball. "Excuse me, sir. I believe that you have something that belongs to me. Sorry about that."

The man twisted to face her. His eyes grew wide. "Wow. The last time I saw you, your ponytail was flying behind you... remember? It was when you abandoned me in Mexico."

Margaret's mouth was too dry to allow her to say much. She simply stared at the man before her—Joe Rohrer. Despite being a tad disheveled from yard work, he was even more handsome than she remembered.

A smile now filled his face. "Margaret Campbell in my backyard? Imagine that. This must be my lucky day."

## Chapter Four

*Later That Afternoon*

*J*oe glanced across the seat at Margaret, admiring the lady as she pointed the blue Land Rover up Pennsylvania Route 23 toward East Earl. "This was nice of you, offering to drive tonight."

She grinned at him. "Well, you did offer to buy dinner if I drove. Sounded like a good deal at the time."

Being with Margaret touched him in a way that was different, yet frighteningly familiar. Margaret was like a breath of fresh air after being cooped up in the office all day—that was the different part. But the scary part was the feeling that was growing in his chest. He'd had this feeling three times before. And while he didn't mind the wonderful warmth of the emotion, it was the eventuality of being dumped that made him sad. Despite the attraction, he needed to keep Margaret at arm's length.

"Are you still cross that I left you behind in Mexico?"

"Kind of. Suppose I would have been arrested?"

She smirked. "But that didn't happen, did it?"

"Well, no. But suppose it did?"

"I see. And what could I have done? Maybe break you out of jail? Wait, I get it. You wanted me to draw them off and be the bait, didn't you?"

"Bait?"

She laughed. "Dr. Rohrer, you're a smart man, aren't you?"

"I'd like to think so, but what does that have to do with what you said?"

"Because the slowest impala becomes supper for the lioness. Were you hoping they would catch me and not you? You know, you could have simply kept up with me."

It was his turn to find humor in the conversation. "Actually, I was thinking you were somewhat of a MacGyver—a girl who could get us out of any jam."

"Wait, is that why you asked me out tonight?" Her eyebrows arched. "Are you thinking about getting in trouble, Joe? Scared some Amishman would best you?"

He intentionally didn't answer and waited for her to glance at him. "Do I look like the type of man who would be scared of anything?"

They were sitting at a light. Margaret's lips were silent as her eyes assessed him. She returned her eyes to the road after the red changed to green.

"I think you're complicated, Joe. Your exterior exudes the confidence of a man in his prime, but your eyes tell a different story. I see a longing for tenderness, for commitment, for surety." She hesitated and chanced a quick glance. "Am I close?"

Joe shook his head. "I see you and Tara have been discussing me."

"Not at all. And I also didn't speak about you to Leslie."

*Leslie?* "What do you mean?"

"Leslie Golden? The designer for Lapp interior. I do believe she's the one you thought I was related to when we met."

It was suddenly very hot in her vehicle. He lowered the window. "How do you know her?"

"Two ways. I hired her to design my showroom and she invited me to be part of the golf foursome today. You remember? When my errant drive ended up in your yard."

*Maybe I should just get out and walk home.* "I didn't know."

"I probably wouldn't have put it together, until Leslie started acting weird after I retrieved my ball. And then at lunch, I remembered she mentioned her sister-in-law Aubrey... with a maiden name of Stettinger."

"Okay. I get it. Why don't we just turn around and head back to my place? You can drop me off along the road."

Margaret pulled over, and then turned to face him. "May I ask why?"

"Because."

Her eyes showed curiosity, and something else. "Can you be more specific?"

"Because you probably think I'm a perv, since you know all about my failures."

"Do you think I'm judging you?"

He looked away and shook his head. "It would be hard not to. Everyone else does. 'Oh, there goes Joe Rohrer, the man no woman wants.' I'm pretty sure that's every woman's thought."

Margaret was silent, so he turned to face her. Margaret's eyes changed and he thought for a moment he detected sadness. Suddenly, she extended her hand. "Hi. My name is Margaret Campbell."

After hesitating briefly, he took her hand. So warm. "What is this about?"

"I wanted to make sure you know who I really am. For the record, I'm a girl who draws my own conclusions. Are we clear on that?"

Joe's mouth was dry. "Yes. Sorry about that."

Her lips turned into a smile. "Still interested in dinner or should I drop you off?"

"Uh, dinner?"

"Good answer. I'm looking forward to Shady Maple *and...* getting to know who you really are."

\*\*\*

Joe watched the fugitive rays of sun finding their way through the blinds. And as he watched their reflection on the blades of the ceiling fan, the image of Margaret's face appeared. Yesterday had been magical. *Who would have thought she would appear, in my backyard?* He recalled their conversation.

*"This must be my lucky day."*

She had smiled but hadn't answered.

*"Maybe you don't remember who I am?"*

*"But I do. Dr. Joseph Rohrer. I'd almost forgotten you lived in Lancaster."*

*"Oh, I'm forgettable?"*

Her smile had grown. *"No, I wouldn't say that."*

The woman who stood next to Margaret touched Margaret's shoulder. *"I'll head back to the course and give you some privacy."*

*"I really should go back too."* Margaret turned to Joe. *"I hate to run, but may I have my golf ball?"*

*"Oh, so you're the one responsible for breaking the mirror on the truck?"*

Her face had paled. *"I'm so sorry. Send me the bill and I'll pay for a new one."*

He had no idea why he had responded the way he did. *"How about we negotiate that over lunch?"*

*"Sorry, we just made plans..."*

Joe's heart tumbled.

*"How about dinner instead?"*

He looked up hopefully. *"I'd love that, but I need to stop at Good's Store before they close. I'm getting some decorations for the yard... wait. I'd love your input. Would you like to go with me?"*

He could see the amusement in her eyes. *"Isn't that store right in front of Shady Maple? Their roast beef and buttered noodles are out of this world."*

*"Sounds like a date."*

He'd never forget her laughter. *"It seems you're a very good negotiator."*

After shopping, they had indeed visited the smorgasbord at Shady Maple before ending up at Stauffer's of Kissel Hill to continue the search for the perfect backyard additions. But the *pièce de résistance* was when she took him to Fox Meadow Creamery in Ephrata for ice cream. However, it wasn't the frozen treat that had been magical. Instead, it was the soft conversation shared between them as they watched the stars appear.

The Kahlua coffee tasted better than he could ever remember. *When was the last time I felt this happy?* He knew the praise for his good mood belonged to the young lady with fair hair.

From the next room, his cell beckoned. Immediately recognizing the ringtone, he answered. "Morning, Daisy."

"Hey! Where were you last night? Jake and I stopped by after the ballgame, but you didn't answer. Were you asleep or running around?"

"Are you sitting down?"

He could sense her confusion. "Wait. Okay, I'm in my recliner now. What's going on?"

His chest was light. "I met her."

"Met who... oh my gosh! Do you mean 'the one'? Are you pulling my leg?"

"No, I'm totally serious. I met her yesterday."

"Wow. Where did this happy event occur?"

*She'll never believe me.* "She walked into my backyard. I turned around and, voila! There she was."

Daisy's voice was muffled. She was obviously talking to her husband. "Jake, Joe met someone."

"Daisy, I didn't just meet anyone, I met *the* one."

"You're on speaker. So, who is she?"

Joe was so excited he could barely contain himself. "Remember when I told you about the girl in Mexico? When I almost got kidnapped?"

Daisy's response was slow. "Vaguely."

But her husband was plainly excited. "Kidnapped? I miss out on all the good stuff. You're seeing a girl who tried to kidnap you?"

Joe couldn't help but laugh. "No, no. We were sharing a cab and this girl, she, she... saved us."

"Sounds like a super-hero. Does she have a cool outfit and a cape, too?"

"Jake, stop making fun of Joe. What's her name?"

Joe took a deep breath. "Margaret Campbell."

He was a little confused by the silence that followed. "As in Tara's sister-in-law? That Margaret Campbell?"

"Well, if you put it that way, yes."

"Joe, I don't mean to burst your bubble, but have you thought this through?"

"There was no need to do that."

"Excuse me? Why not?"

"You see, I got it on good advice... this time everything will work out."

"Who's the idiot who gave you that advice?"

Joe ran his hand through his hair. "Don't you remember? You did, Daisy."

## Chapter Five

*Two Weeks Later*

Margaret removed the final bottle of wine from the cork press, wiped it off and passed it to Rebecca Stoltzfus. The Amish girl placed the glass container in the wooden crate. "That was the last one."

Isaac Golden handed cold bottles of water to the two women. "I think a celebration is in order. You know, something to honor this special occasion. The Scottish Lass's first bottling run." He grinned at Margaret.

Rebecca seemed confused. "Shouldn't you celebrate by tasting the wine?"

Margaret smiled. "Hmm. The longer it ages, the better it will taste, but... wait right here." She walked away, but reappeared quickly. In her hands were three goblets, each half-filled with a light, rose colored wine. "There wasn't enough to fill another bottle, but there was some for each of us to raise a toast." Margaret handed Isaac one glass, then offered the other to Rebecca.

Rebecca stared at it and then took a deep breath. "I-I'm not really sure if I should. I've never had alcohol."

"Oh, I wasn't trying to tempt you. Sorry about that."

The girl turned to Isaac. "If I only take one sip, will that make me drunk?"

Margaret had noticed it several times previously. It was easy to see there was a bond between the two. Not a romantic connection, but one similar to siblings. Rebecca had asked Isaac for advice a couple of times. "It's up to you, but I don't think a sip will hurt. After all, it's not every day you commemorate the first batch of wine in a new winery."

Rebecca smiled at Isaac and then turned back to Margaret. "Well then, I'll celebrate with you, but just this once."

Margaret held her glass high. "Here's to the success of the Scottish Lass. And to the two friends who've helped make this inaugural run possible."

The three of them clinked glasses and proceeded to raise the wine to their mouths. Isaac emptied his in one quick gulp, as if it were water, then wiped his mouth with his arm. However, the Amish girl only allowed a tiny splash to touch her lips before lowering the glass.

Rebecca turned to Margaret. "Oh my! It tastes like strawberries, but it makes my mouth tingly." She shifted her gaze to Isaac. "Did it tickle your lips, too?"

"Did it make his lips do what?" They all twisted to see the owner of the voice. "Why are the three of you drinking in the afternoon and at work, no less?" Leslie Golden stood, hands on her hips, as she surveyed them. The woman's icy gaze fell on Rebecca.

Margaret wiped her mouth with her fingers. "We just finished corking the first batch of strawberry wine. I named it Spring Blush. I'll send a bottle home with you."

"How kind of you." All of Leslie's attention was focused on the girl in the black dress. Rebecca extended her arm and offered up her glass. The girl's voice was uneven as she spoke. "W-we were tasting M-M-Miss Campbell's first wine bottling. Here, you can have the rest of mine."

The young girl's face was now bright red, as if she were a child caught red-handed while doing something wrong.

Leslie stepped closer and glared at the Amish girl. "I didn't think you were old enough to drink. Refresh my memory. How old are you, Becky?"

"N-nineteen. And please don't call me Becky. My given name is Rebecca."

"Nineteen, huh? And let me guess, you were named after the Rebecca from the Bible?"

The girl nodded. "I think so."

Leslie's eyes were icy. "Rebecca, hmm. Wasn't she the mother of Jacob and Esau? One of the Bible's most deceitful women. She helped Jacob steal Esau's birthright, if I remember. Is that correct?"

Rebecca stuttered as she answered. "Y-y-yes, M-M-Mrs. G-g-golden."

Leslie shook her head. "Rebecca was Isaac's wife. In the *Old* Testament." The other girl's face turned dark, dark red. Leslie snatched the glass from the girl. "Becky, are you aware you just broke the law? In Pennsylvania, you have to be twenty-one to drink. Or maybe the laws don't apply because you're

Amish, huh?" Leslie drained the glass in one quick gulp, but then started to cough.

Isaac was quickly by his wife's side. "Leslie, what's wrong? Are you okay?" He patted her back.

Margaret struggled not to smirk. *Ah, karma. God's paying you back for treating Rebecca so harshly.*

Leslie spoke between attempts to breathe. "Swallowed... wrong... went down... went down the wrong pipe." Finally, her breathing returned to normal. Leslie's eyes found Margaret's. "Came to check on the progress downstairs. Care to join me?" Leslie's head motioned to the stairs.

Now Margaret felt like *she* was the schoolgirl who'd been naughty and the teacher was calling her to the hallway for a scolding. "Give me a minute." Her attention moved to Isaac and Rebecca. "Thank you again for your help today. Would you two mind taking the bottles into the catacomb? I'll be back shortly and we'll go over how to clean the equipment."

Leslie's lips were set in a fine white line as Margaret followed her down the stairs to the first floor and into the shop. The walls had been freshly painted and the grids were on the windows. Boxes of trim sat along the room's exterior beneath the windows.

Margaret took a deep breath. "Looks like it's coming along nicely."

Leslie pivoted and faced Margaret. "I suppose you want to know why I acted the way I did upstairs."

*I hate when people put others down so they can feel superior.* "I believe I've got it narrowed down.

Either you're jealous or you dislike my female employee."

Leslie physically took a step backwards. "You don't know her. She tried to trick Devo into marrying her last year and from what I saw upstairs, she's at it again. That girl is devious."

"Hmm, I thought they both acted very professionally. Rebecca and Isaac work well together and they displayed something to each other you certainly don't show—*respect*."

Leslie shook her head. "Oh, you don't know that girl or her intentions. She has her sights set on *my* husband. Under that white cap dwells an evil woman."

Margaret shook her head. "Wow. Tell me. What's it like to be clairvoyant?"

Leslie either didn't hear or ignored Margaret. "I don't want her working with him. In the future, I'd appreciate if you—"

Margaret raised her hands. "Enough! Stop, right there. This is my business and no one tells me what to do."

Leslie's face began to turn pink. "What does that mean? I thought we were friends."

"We are, but don't think you can tell me how to manage my business."

Margaret could almost see the wheels turning in Leslie's mind. "Why was my husband here in the first place? He's a mechanic, not a laborer like her. Something smells fishy. Did she ask for him to come over and work with her?"

"Leslie. With all due respect, you're stepping over the line. I'll explain, but only in the interest of our friendship. The reason Isaac was here is because I was having trouble with the equipment. It was the first time we'd used it and your husband had to make numerous adjustments."

Leslie took a deep breath. "I'm sorry. It's just that Becky has been a thorn in my side. I really don't trust her."

Margaret patted her friend's shoulder. "Then trust your husband. I don't know him all that well, but I can assure you, that man loves you. Everyone, including Rebecca, can see that."

The other woman nodded. Leslie's color was returning to normal as she calmed down. "I know. It's just that I waited all my life for the right man and I guess you're right. I did overreact."

"Yes, you did. And I want you to apologize to Rebecca."

Leslie's mouth dropped open. "Apologize? Why?"

"For two reasons. First, I don't want anyone to feel this is a hostile work place. But more importantly, I think you owe it to Isaac. When you were yelling at her, I saw the disappointment in his eyes. Isaac needs to know you trust him."

Leslie pursed her lips. "How did you get to be so smart and know so much about relationships? Did you study psychology in college?"

Margaret smiled. "No. I'm just observant. Something my brother Henry taught me. Now, unless there's anything else you want to discuss, should we check out the showroom's progress?"

Leslie glanced at the door to the catacomb. "Give me a moment. I need to apologize to Devo... and Becky, I, uh, mean, Rebecca first."

\*\*\*

Ellie waddled over to the zero-gravity chair. She waved when she saw her best friend, Sophie Miller, walk out the door of the house next door. Sophie's four sons surrounded her. Ellie's own quartet of daughters ran across the yard to greet them. Ben Miller, her friend's husband, pulled a wagon laden with chairs and dishes.

Ellie struggled to her feet and hugged Sophie. "Hey, I haven't seen you all week."

"Missed you, Ellie. These days are extremely busy."

"At home or at the tea room?"

Sophie rolled her eyes and replied, "Both."

Ben walked over until he stood at his wife's side. He reached down and kissed Ellie's cheek. "Hi, El. You look lovely this evening." Ellie gave Ben a peck in return.

Ellie could see the teasing in Sophie's eyes as she playfully smacked her husband's arm. "Why don't you ever say anything like that to me?"

Ben quickly grabbed Sophie, supporting her back as he dipped her and planted a romantic kiss on her lips. He pulled away. "Woman, if you don't know how I feel about you and how much I love you by now, you never will."

From the corner of her eye, Ellie observed Henry and Margaret emerge from the side of their house. Henry toted a tray laden with food while his sister lugged gallon jugs of lemonade, iced tea and milk.

Henry hailed the Millers. "Isn't it a beautiful evening? I hope everyone brought their appetites. I'll be grilling plenty of burgers and hot dogs."

Ben hurried over and took the drinks from Margaret. "I haven't seen you since your homecoming party. Are you getting settled in?"

Ellie couldn't miss her sister-in-law's smile, but picked up a hint of sadness in it. Sophie shuffled over and hugged Margaret tightly. "I'm so glad you moved home. Maybe we'll get a chance to have more time together."

"That would be nice."

By now, Henry had deposited the tray onto a table. He approached the group and Sophie reached for him. Ellie saw Margaret recoil when Sophie and Henry kissed on the lips. Ben caught Ellie's glance and shook his head with a smile. The two of them had grown accustomed to the strange method their spouses used to greet each other. And more importantly, they understood why.

"Have you met our sons?" Ben asked Margaret, motioning to the boys. "Hey, Miller boys! Front and center. I want to introduce you to Auntie Margaret."

The boys' red hair and freckled cheeks were warning indicators of the trouble they could get into. While the four brothers were wild around Sophie, they listened to Ben without fail. Margaret stood there, eyes taking in the children. A slight chill dribbled down Ellie's spine. *Something's wrong.* Ellie couldn't quite identify the expression on her sister-in-law's face.

The time together passed quickly and it was soon time for a bath and bedtime stories. The Millers bid everyone farewell and headed home. Ellie was particularly tired this evening and Henry must have sensed Ellie's exhaustion. He approached, two daughters in each arm. "How about I take care of bathing our princesses this evening? You deserve a break."

"Would you mind?"

"Absolutely not, honey." Henry leaned down and slowly kissed Ellie. "I love you. If you're not in by the time we're ready to read stories, I'll send little Maggie May out for you. I know how precious these days are." He kissed Ellie again before leaving.

The sun was low in the sky, but hadn't yet set. To the west, a hot air balloon floated along the horizon. The sweet scent of the watermelon they had eaten for dessert lingered in the evening air. Margaret took the chair next to Ellie. The younger woman seemed reflective.

"How are you doing? Since you came back, I haven't seen very much of you."

Margaret's eyes seemed focused to the east. "I've been really busy."

"And how's the vineyard coming?"

"We bottled three runs of fruit wine this week. Still working out the kinks."

Ellie touched the girl's hand. "I'm so proud of you, chasing your dreams. And I'm glad you're home." Margaret's expression didn't change. "Are you glad to be back in Paradise?"

Her sister-in-law shrugged. "I don't know."

*Why is she so sad?* "What do you mean?"

"Everything's changed."

"I don't understand. What do you mean?"

"The family's different. Harry has Ashley and his books. Edmund and Tara have their girls. Mum has a life all of her own and runs around all the time. And you and Henry..."

*She's lonely.* "I'm sorry."

"While I was away, life moved on without me. Things aren't at all like they used to be. I miss the old days and the life we all used to share."

"Henry and I will make more of an effort to include you in things. We could—"

Margaret turned to Ellie with a swiftness that surprised her. "Can I ask you a question?"

"Of course."

"Are you happy?"

*Where did that come from?* "Absolutely. Why do you ask?"

Margaret's eyes were like laser beams, scanning Ellie's heart and soul. "I remember when you were missing. The police told us you were dead. But Henry shared with me how he could feel you in his heart and said it was reciprocal, that you could feel him as well and knew we would find you. And after we rescued you, I recall seeing it first-hand and thinking how lucky you two were. Your happiness and love could easily be seen. Undeniably, I witnessed true love. Do you two still feel the same?"

"Yes. The closeness, the connection... it's still like that. We're very happy."

"Really?"

"Why, of course."

Margaret stood and didn't make eye contact. "I believe you feel like that, Ellie. But I'm not so sure Henry does. Sorry, just forget it. Good night."

## Chapter Six

*Tuesday Evening*

Joe turned the Camaro into his drive. It had been a long day at the practice and he was late getting home. Margaret was supposed to drop by this evening so they could go out. His friend had hinted she was hungry for Italian food.

The sight of that bright blue Land Rover sitting in front of his garage made his chest tingle. *She's here.* He found the beauty sitting on his front step. The fair-haired damsel stood and waved. Despite her smile, he could sense something was wrong. Worry started to nag at the back of his mind.

He parked next to her SUV and got out. She walked to him and much to his surprise, wrapped her arms around him. Joe didn't resist and held her tightly. While the faint aroma of grapes surrounded Margaret, the wonderful sensation of her embrace melted away his every care in the world. "What a pleasant way to come home, seeing you." *A guy could get used to this.*

"I missed you, Joe."

"As I did you."

He had to be careful here. *This time is going to be different.* This lady was something special and Joe needed to do this right. *No rushing this time.* He was hoping they could build a close friendship and then, with a little luck, Margaret would realize she was in love with him. She squeezed him even tighter.

"Everything okay?" he asked.

She released him with a sigh. "Mind if we just stay here tonight instead of going out?"

*Don't care where we are, as long as we're together.* "Not at all. I can throw something on the grill or we can call out... whatever you prefer."

She motioned to a cooler sitting on the steps. "I had Rebecca Stoltzfus pick up a few things for me at Roots today. I ordered a couple of real Italian subs and also had her buy a ham loaf for later this week, if that's okay. For tonight, I was kind of hoping we could have a picnic... you know, in that masterpiece garden of yours."

He laughed as he opened the front door for her. "It only looks as well as it does because of your flair for lawn decorations."

"True, true." She closed her eyes and seemed to be enjoying the air conditioning. But a sudden change of expression concerned him. "I need to tell you something."

The temperature in the room must have dropped a hundred degrees. He shivered. *Please no. I don't want to lose you, too.* "What is that, Margaret?"

She took his hands and faced him.

"First, can you call me Maggie from now on?"

"Of, of c-course. I thought you only wanted to be called Margaret."

Sadness seemed to flow and form an aura of sorrow around her. "My family calls me Margaret. But it's time I changed. I want my dearest friends to call me Maggie from now on."

*Dearest friends... like me?* YES! "Alright, *Maggie*. What did you want to tell me?"

Her hands were fidgety and her eyes studied his carpet. "I'm having some... some issues at home. I don't think I can stay there anymore."

"Issues? What happened?"

Margaret took a deep breath. "Everything changed while I was gone. And then my stupid brother..."

He held her hands and waited. "What about your brother?" Joe was surprised by her sob.

"He's just not the man I thought he was. I've lost my respect for Henry, and, and... I just don't want to be around him anymore. It's bad enough we co-own the business, but, but I just can't live under the same roof as him from now on."

*Must be so hard for her.* "What can I do to help?"

"I've never bought a house. I could use your advice and guidance."

Joe's mouth went dry. *My greatest hope is to share a home with you, someday.* "I'll help any way that I can. How soon are you looking to move?"

Those green eyes were so beautiful. "As soon as I can. I don't want to be living there when everything comes apart."

"Comes apart? Exactly what happened?"

"It, it's a long story, and I'm pretty hungry. Would you mind if we ate soon?"

Joe's curiosity was almost killing him. *Don't push. Let her tell you in time.* "Of course. I have some veggies I could grill to go along with those subs. How's that sound?"

"Perfect." Margaret reached for his hands. "Joe, thank you."

He couldn't help but smile. "For what? Are you already anticipating my master grilling skills?"

She nodded. "Well, I am, but that's not what I meant. Thank you for... well, just being such a great friend. For not thinking I'm crazy and telling me what to do. I hate when people do that."

He drew her into a warm hug this time. "I'll never do that."

She squeezed him very tightly. "I'm so lucky to have you as my friend."

"I'm the fortunate one. And I promise you, Maggie, I'll always be here, right by your side."

Her smile was the most beautiful sight he'd ever seen. "I'm really beginning to hope so."

***

Didi coaxed the horse to speed up so she and Margaret could ride side by side. "This is so kind, letting me ride your horse."

Margaret's gaze seemed fixed on the girls playing in the backyard. "It's my pleasure." She shook her head. "I like being outdoors. Never was one of those stay in the house type of women. Guess that's why I liked California."

There was such a sad aura surrounding Margaret tonight. "Is everything okay?"

"Why would you ask?"

"I don't know. You seem a little down, that's all."

Margaret turned to face Didi. "You've got a sharp eye for things. Must be the reporter in you."

"Would you like to talk about it?"

"Hi, ladies." Didi turned to the source of the female voice. Henry Campbell and his wife Ellie were standing in the yard with the kids. Didi noticed Margaret increase her horse's gait and head for open pasture.

"Evening, you two. How is the Campbell family tonight?"

Ellie answered. "We're fine. Where's LBJ?"

The pair were always so kind to Didi and her son. "He's with my parents tonight. Maggie and I are taking an evening ride."

Henry looked confused. "Maggie? Or did you mean Maggot?"

"Why would I call her Maggot?"

"Never mind. If you were talking about my sister, she goes by Margaret. Maggie is our daughter."

"Hmm. That's what she told me to call her... starting tonight. That's what she said."

The married couple shared a confused look. Ellie shrugged and returned her attention to Didi. "Next time you come over, bring LBJ. He can have a play date with our girls." The lady pointed to Margaret's retreating figure. "You'll have to hurry if you want to get caught up with my sister-in-law. Nice seeing you again."

"You as well. Good night."

Didi spurred her horse to a gallop. Even so, it took almost five minutes to catch up. She pulled back the reins to match the speed of Margaret's horse. "Maggie, slow down. Are you in a hurry to get somewhere?"

The fair-haired woman pointed to a small copse of trees that sat along the creek. "Let's stop here and let the horses take a drink." Both women dismounted and found a place to sit among the reeds.

Margaret was silent, watching the water spiders dance along the surface of the slow-moving creek. "You're awfully quiet this evening. Want to talk?"

"There's a lot weighing on my mind, that's all."

Didi studied her. "Does it have something to do with your family?" Margaret's nod was slow. "I'm here, if you want to talk. Or, if you just want someone to hang out with, that's okay, too."

"I'd appreciate that."

Luke's face suddenly flashed before her. Even though her husband had been missing for almost three years, she could still feel him.

They sat in silence, watching the horses nibble on the clumps of orchard grass.

Didi was surprised when Margaret started to speak. "Did you ever have a dream that you worked so hard for, but when you achieved it, the reality was so much less than the fantasy you'd created in your mind?"

"Are you talking about your vineyard?"

"No. I was talking about my family."

"Go on."

"From the time I was a wee lass, I drew my strength from my mother and brothers. I looked up to them. Respected them, well, maybe Edmund not so much." Margaret waved her hand to chase a fly away. "My brother Harry and I had a secret, his writing. We were very close. In the old days, he used to drive up to State College every Wednesday to see me. But now he's married to Ashley and it's like I no longer exist."

Didi's mind traveled back in time to her youth. Even though her home was filled with love, she'd missed having a brother or a sister. "I was an only child. I can only imagine how special that was."

Margaret brushed her hand across her cheek. "Edmund and I were never really close, but we had some good memories. My brother Henry, he stepped up when Pops died. Henry became my father figure, the rock of the family. A man of truth and honesty." She stopped for a few seconds. "You could always depend on old Henry. I used to be scared of thunder and lightning storms. He'd let me come to his room and he'd hold me until it passed. Felt so safe and protected. I had so much respect for him. So faithful to the family."

Didi touched her arm. "I can believe that. He and Ellie stop by from time to time, to bring us fresh vegetables. And Henry seems to know when my anxieties are running out of control. Always has a kind word to say, to keep my faith up that they'll find Luke and bring him home."

Her companion shook her head. "Do you know the story about Ellie and Henry?"

"No."

Margaret shared how the two had met and about their bond of nonverbal communication, even when Ellie was presumed dead.

A chill rolled across Didi's shoulders. "What do you mean?"

"Ellie disappeared. The police believed she'd been murdered, but Henry said he could feel she was alive."

The chill increased. This sounded familiar. *Like I feel Luke is still alive, somewhere, not only in my heart.* "That must have been horrible."

"It was. I flew to Hawaii and joined Henry. For weeks we searched for her all day, every day, even after her family gave up hope and believed she was gone forever." Margaret palmed her eyes with the base of her hand. "Then one morning I woke to find Henry despondent. Told me Ellie had given up hope. I prayed for a miracle and God granted one. That day, He led me to the clue we needed."

"What was that?"

"In a filthy little shop, I saw a man pawn Ellie's necklace—the one she still wears today. I called Henry. Oh, the man didn't want to tell us anything, but my brother can be quite persuasive. We raided the island where Ellie was being held captive."

Didi's mouth dropped open. "You? As in you and Henry?"

"Um-hmm. We got her off that wretched island and Henry played a game of cat and mouse with the kidnappers until the Navy showed up." Margaret dabbed at her eyes again. "They shot Henry... almost killed him."

"I'm glad they didn't."

Margaret didn't appear to hear. "I watched the love between Ellie and Henry grow. It made me wish someday I would find true love, like they had."

Didi smiled. "They are like the perfect couple. A perfect example of what love is supposed to be."

Her friend's face turned dark. "I thought so, too... until I discovered the truth."

"The truth? What truth?"

"My brother is the most despicable man in the world. I can't even stand being in the same room as him. I feel angry, betrayed. And that's why I need to find somewhere else to live."

"Maggie, I don't understand."

"Didi, my brother is a liar and... a cheat."

## *Chapter Seven*

*A Summer Sunday Afternoon*

The heat of the day was oppressive, but Joe would gladly walk through Hell itself just to be with Maggie. They were hiking along the rail trail in York County, just south of Brillhart Station. He took a swig of water and wiped the sweat from his brow. "Doesn't the heat bother you?"

She stopped and turned to him. "Sorry. Was I walking too fast?"

"No, but you do seem to be in a hurry. Are you sure you have time for this today?"

Those brilliant green eyes normally had a fire behind them, but they were subdued this afternoon. "There's no place else I'd rather be. I enjoy our friendship and didn't mean to leave you behind."

"That's okay." Time for the sixty-four-thousand-dollar question. "What's bothering you?"

Margaret was silent as she searched his face. A drop of sweat ran down his nose. He wiped it away. "Can you keep a secret?"

*Tell me you're in love with me.* "Absolutely."

"Someone I used to love and respect... he hurt me deeply."

A chilling sensation rolled over him despite the heat. *She's grieving the loss of a lover.* "I had the utmost admiration for him, but he's not at all what he appeared to be." The shrill ring of a bike's bell broke their attention. They stepped aside to allow a string of bikers to speed past. "Let's walk and talk. Perhaps this landmark you told me about will lift my spirits."

"Sure." She was so close. He wanted to slip his arm around Margaret's waist and pull her close, but he sensed she needed his ear more than any other part. "I'm here for you." *And hopefully always will be.*

A small ravine opened on the left. Squirrels were playing tag amongst the leaves. "Do you believe in true love, like there's only one man for only one woman and God predestined it when He made the world?"

The chill grew. *She's mourning.* "I do. And you do as well?"

She grimaced. "I used to. When I saw them together for the first time, I believed it was indeed true love. They belonged together. All part of God's plan. And my heart was so happy for him."

A woman ran toward them, pushing one of those three-wheeled jogging carriages in front of her. The little girl within was sporting sunglasses and holding a Winnie-the-Pooh stuffed animal as she bounced along. Joe nodded as the pair passed them. "Are you still happy for him?"

Margaret snorted. "Not anymore. I'm pretty sure he is one of the most blessed men on this planet. Successful business, a beautiful, loving and devoted wife, gorgeous daughters… everything anyone could want… and like an idiot, he's throwing it away." She sniffled, which all but broke Joe's heart. "Yet he has everyone fooled." She palmed her eyes. "And for whatever reason, I'm the only one who sees it."

He didn't understand the pain in her voice. Was she sad because this person was with someone else, or perhaps because this man from her past was flawed? "What do you see?"

"How he has everyone fooled into believing he's wonderful, yet still does whatever he chooses. And his poor wife is oblivious to it all. She's still caught up with a dewy-eyed belief they're living in some fairytale. And he has the gall to flaunt it right before her. I know and respect his wife. She's one of the smartest women I've ever met, but he has the wool pulled over her eyes. She doesn't see it."

Margaret hesitated as they continued to walk in silence along the trail, now passing over the Codorus Creek. Joe remained silent. Joe understood how it could hurt, reliving the past, but talking about it helped. He knew that from personal experience. Joe had cried more than once on his friend Daisy's shoulder. Maggie needed to get this out in the open—it was where true healing began.

Two young men walked by, loudly discussing a baseball game. After they passed, Margaret spoke. "I've loved him forever, but this time, he's gone overboard. Mark my words, his luck is going to run out. And he's so cavalier about it." She suddenly stopped, grabbed Joe's arm and spun him toward her. "Do you know, I even saw him kiss her in front of his wife and the other woman's husband... on the lips... like he didn't even care. Like he just knew he could get away with whatever he damned well wanted to do."

It was hard to follow this. "Kissed who?"

"The other woman. Would you believe she's his neighbor, no less? And I don't understand why no one else notices this. Don't get me started on his betrayal, but then when I look at her children, it's so plain."

The agony in her face made his own heart hurt. Joe swept the hair from her face. "What's so obvious?"

Margaret grasped his arms tightly. "He's the father of his neighbor's children. The resemblance is undeniable. I can't be the only one to notice it."

She began to walk along the trail, but Margaret still held his hand. "I think the thing that hurts the most is what he took from me."

Joe shook his head. *I believe I know what he stole from you, Margaret.* He well understood her misery, and the heartbreak of being betrayed. "And that is?"

"He took away my innocence, my belief in true love... my faith in men." She sniffled as they walked. "And most likely my ability to ever love again."

The grade of the railway was flattening out. They passed the final turn and the tunnel was right there before them. He'd looked forward to revealing Howard Tunnel to her, but Margaret was too buried in the past right now. He was the one who stopped and moved her so they faced each other. He opened his arms and she slipped into his embrace. Her sorrow overflowed onto the shoulder of his shirt.

People passing by on bikes or walking stared at them. Joe didn't care. This was a necessary moment. Margaret had to get rid of this grief so she could move on. Time no longer mattered as he held her close. Finally, she released him and wiped her eyes with her forearms. "Some blubbering mess I am, huh? You'll probably never want to be seen with the likes of me again."

"I wouldn't care if the whole world was watching. I'm here for you, Maggie." The emotion was rising in him. *Tell her how you feel!* "I plan on always being here with you."

Her smile touched him, especially in the way those eyes shined. "You are special, Joseph Rohrer. I'm glad we're close friends." Her lips suddenly brushed his cheek. Before he could react and press his mouth to hers—which is what he'd been wanting to do since he'd met her in Mexico—she moved her attention to the landscape. "So, is this the tunnel you were telling me about? How marvelous."

*I need to tell her.* He hadn't moved. Their hands were still clasped together. He gently tugged until their eyes met. "I'm glad it wasn't you."

The girl's brows raised. "Wasn't me? What do you mean?"

"I'm glad you're not with him... and that it isn't you he's unfaithful to."

Her face turned bright pink. She nodded and he realized this was an "ah-ha" moment. *Please read between the lines and take notice how much I care.*

She touched his nose with her finger. "You misunderstood me. I'm not talking about an old lover. The man who ruined my faith in men was someone else. It's my brother... Henry."

\*\*\*

Margaret sensed Joe's hesitation as they walked across the parking lot. *I know why.* He was holding an umbrella above her head to ward off the rain. "Look, we don't have to do this if you really don't want to."

He shook his head. "No, I don't mind."

*He's such a wonderful friend.* "Liar. You're uncomfortable because Sophie is Tara's sister-in-law and this is Sophie's tea room."

Joe stared at her. "Am I that easy to read?"

"No. I simply listen to you."

"With the memory of an elephant! I told you about Tara last year when we were in Mexico."

It was time to tease him a little. "You also told me about Leslie and Aubrey that day as well."

His smile was now a frown. "I've read about people like you... you've got some sort of photographic mind complex thing going for you, don't you?"

"No, just an eye for detail... for what's important... to people who mean a lot to me." Margaret topped that off with a playful wink.

Joe's cheeks blushed as he stood there. The look of wonder in his eyes gave him away. She'd sensed for a while that Joe cared for her, deeply, but had avoided it. *Is it love I see there?* He touched her arm. "Maggie, can I ask..."

*I can't allow myself to... not yet. My teasing's leading down the wrong path.* The conversation was suddenly too much, way too personal because of the thoughts trying to surface. She was attracted to Joe in a way she'd forbidden herself from feeling. But there was no time for romance in her life, not right now. "No. Let's focus on the task at hand. We can leave if you'd like."

The man sighed and looked away. "Nope. You asked me for my opinion, so let's do it."

He walked ahead and the bell tinkled when he opened the door. Margaret glanced around the shop while Joe stowed the umbrella. Margaret was glad Sophie wasn't at her usual place behind the podium, but she really hadn't expected her to be. Margaret had overheard Henry and Ellie talking about meeting the Millers here for tea this evening before they headed off to a show at the American Music Theater. Today's timing had been just perfect. Margaret's sister-in-law, Ashley, also worked here, but had the day off. Hopefully Margaret and Joe would be able to quickly leave afterwards without notice.

The tea room was unusually packed for this late in the day. Luckily, the corner table where they were seated provided an excellent line of sight of the entire tea room. They'd have a good view of the scene.

Joe glanced at the menu. "Refresh my memory, will it be tea and crumpets or are we getting sandwiches? I'm starved, by the way."

"I wish you'd learn to listen to me as well as I listen to you. We're only having a snack here. I promised I'd treat for supper later." She extracted her phone, unlocked the screen and handed it to Joe. "Check out this photo."

Joe studied the image. "Okay. I take it the four boys are Ben and Sophie's sons."

Margaret nodded. "In a manner of speaking. Now swipe to the next picture—the one of Henry as a lad. See the resemblance?"

His eyes widened as he swiped back and forth between the two. "I see what you're saying. The resemblance is uncanny. The hair color, the eyes, cheekbones, chin... remarkable." His eyes met hers. "But Henry Campbell? I can't picture him cheating on Ellie."

"Answer me this. Do you think Sophie Miller is pretty?"

"Of course. She's drop dead gorgeous and, don't get offended, but she has like the perfect figure, I mean when she isn't pregnant..."

"No offense taken." From the corner of her eye, she recognized the Millers' vehicle turn into the lot.

"And Ellie? Is she prettier or more attractive than Sophie?"

He shook his head. "Why do I feel there's no right answer here?"

"I asked for your opinion."

He squinted before answering. "I can believe most men would prefer a woman like Sophie over Ellie, on looks alone. But your sister-in-law has the grace of royalty and a heart of gold. Sophie's nice, but couldn't hold a candle to Ellie's personality."

"I believe what you've said, Dr. Rohrer, on looks alone, it would be a landslide. Do you concur?"

"Yes, but Henry is married to Ellie. Surely you don't think..." His voice trailed off.

"Yes, I do. And for the record, even royals stray occasionally. Shh, Sophie and Ben just walked in."

The two conspirators kept their heads down until the Millers were seated. The pair had the premier table in the tea room. It overlooked the garden.

Margaret didn't have to wait long before her brother and his wife arrived. Ever the perfect gentleman, or so he pretended to be in public, Henry held the umbrella for Ellie while they crossed the lot. Once again, Margaret and Joe kept their heads low to avoid detection when her brother and his wife passed nearby.

Margaret's voice was a low whisper. "Watch closely and keep an eye on the greeting."

Margaret hid behind her teacup. Both Sophie and Ben stood as the other couple approached. Sophie extended her arms and hugged Ellie. No sooner had Sophie released Henry's wife when Ben gave Ellie a kiss on the cheek. But while that was going on, Sophie stepped toward Henry, reached for him and drew him against her body. After a hug warm enough to melt four glaciers, Sophie pursed her lips and was met by Henry. The kiss lasted maybe all of two seconds, but Margaret didn't miss the joy in Sophie's eyes or the way she touched Henry's nose, winking at him afterwards.

"Did you see that?"

When Joe didn't answer, she turned to him. He was shaking his head in apparent disbelief. "I thought you were exaggerating, Maggie. I can't believe my own eyes. Kissing like that in public, right in front of their spouses. How could Ellie and Ben not see it?"

"Maybe there's more here than meets the eye."

"I don't understand."

"Something Ellie once told me... No, it couldn't be true. Not Ellie. She, she wouldn't. I respect her too much to even consider it."

"Consider what?"

Margaret drained her teacup and dropped a pair of twenties on the table. "Not here. Let's leave before our luck runs out."

Joe followed her outside. Margaret was in such a hurry that she didn't even wait for Joe to get the umbrella open before running to his car. She stood in the pouring rain, pausing only until he powered the locks open.

Joe crawled in next to her and reached for her hands. His were warm, but hers were cold... and shaking. "Maggie, you're scaring me. Something startled you. What was it?"

Her chest ached as if someone had stabbed her. *I used to look up to them.* "Ellie... she once told me about Ben."

"What about Ben?"

"And this might explain why they look the other way when Henry and Sophie kiss."

"I'm not following you."

"In college... Ellie and Ben were lovers."

## Chapter Eight

*A Few Days Later*

llie eased into the chair with Henry's help. The baby was very active tonight, making Ellie uncomfortable. Removing the smart phone from her pocket, she swiped and brought up the nanny cameras. "Looks like our girls are all asleep."

"Good. I'm pretty sure if we'd watched even one more minute of *The Little Mermaid*, I would have jumped out of the window. My fun meter's about pegged."

Even though he was complaining, Ellie could feel his mirth. Ever since they'd met, she and Henry shared an unexplainable ability to read each other's feelings and occasionally minds as well. And that gift brought a sense of joined intimacy Ellie never imagined existed. "I know you love being a daddy of princesses, my king."

His tired smile was so appealing. "You know me well, my queen."

"Precisely as well as you know me." He reached for her hand as they watched the stars appear. She pointed to a bright object just above the rim of the horizon. "Look, there's Venus."

"How do you know it's not Mars?"

"Because Venus is bright, happy and elegant, whereas Mars is confused, angry and red."

Henry turned and cocked his eyebrow. "And you can tell that just by looking at them?"

She could feel her dimples appear as she smiled. "Do you mean to tell me you can't sense that as well?"

"Of course not. I think women have an ability to simply look at things and assess them for exactly what they are. It's an unfair advantage over men, if you think about it. And I wouldn't mind if it was just you, but I do believe other women have the same gift."

"Other women? Like who?"

"Hmm, there's you and Mum, for example. When I was a wee one and did something bad, she could sense it from three counties away. I believe once or twice she punished me for something that I'd thought about, but hadn't yet occurred. And then Mum took a spoon to my hide because she suspected I would commit the crime in the future."

"Imagine that... You know who else is good at it?"

He studied her face and Ellie knew he was trying to read her mind. A smile slowly appeared in the growing dusk. "My brother Harry's wife, Ashley."

She couldn't contain her giggle. Even though his guess was incorrect. Henry had such a way of touching her deep inside. "I wasn't thinking of our sister-in-law. Instead, I was thinking of your sister." His smile faded and she sensed his disappointment.

"I wouldn't know. It seems my little Maggot isn't the same girl she used to be. And for whatever reason, she no longer likes her eldest brother."

Ellie squeezed his hand. Since the death of his Pops, Henry not only acted as the patriarch in the family, he'd devoted his life to their happiness. That was why he moved them all to America. Henry had insisted the home Ellie shared with him had to be big enough so they and their families could all live under one roof together.

"The world has changed since we first moved here. All three of you brothers are married now and we're all busy with our own individual lives. It's simply not fair of Margaret to expect her family to put their lives on hold until she decided to move home."

"How do you think she'll react when we tell her we're building a new house?"

Ellie shrugged. "I'm not so sure she'll care. I don't think she really likes living with us anymore. I guess our dream about the entire family living together under one roof wasn't realistic, was it?"

"Probably not, but converting this place into a bed and breakfast will be perfect. Each of the ten bedrooms has a private bath. There's both indoor and outdoor hot tubs and I'll miss that fireplace. We simply have to have one in the family room when we design the new place. And of course, our bedroom will have both a fireplace and a hot tub." She felt the teasing before he said a word. Even in the near dark, she saw him rub his left arm—right where he'd been shot the night when he freed her from her kidnappers. "Simply for medicinal purposes, you know."

Ellie giggled at the man squeezing her hand. "I see. It will be sad not having Ben and Sophie right next door, though. I love how they're always here or we're over there."

"I believe no matter where we live, the Millers will always find a reason to come over." He lowered his voice and muttered, "Sometimes they remind me of a bad penny that keeps showing up."

"Hmm. Now getting back to your sister... when were you planning on telling her we're moving?"

"I'd hoped to bring it up at our family dinners, but she's missed the last two. I don't know if you've taken notice, but she seems to be avoiding me like the plague. Where do you think she goes every evening?"

Ellie suddenly missed Margaret, and how close they'd once been. *Why'd we drift apart?* "Maybe she has a boyfriend."

"I find that hard to believe. Ellie, I've never even known her to date, even when we lived in Scotland. She's always been focused on her dreams... too busy for love. I've kind of suspected Margaret would end up being an old maid."

"Do you remember the night she and Didi went horseback riding? How Didi said Margaret wanted to be called Maggie? What's that about?"

"I don't know. What does your woman's intuition think is going on?"

A soft crying sound caught her attention. Ellie checked her smart phone. Their youngest was sitting up in bed, rubbing her eyes. Before Ellie could say a word, Henry stood. "I'll go see what's wrong. Why don't you just rest? Back in a jiffy." Her husband kissed her and headed for the house. The child within jumped precisely when Henry's lips touched hers. Henry sure had a way of moving "his girls." Ellie was certain she was carrying her fifth daughter, not her first son. *Go figure...*

Ellie's mind drifted back to Margaret. *Something's not right with her.* But Ellie didn't quite know what it was and she definitely didn't want to worry Henry by sharing her thoughts. He had enough on his mind right now. Margaret's face appeared in Ellie's mind and it wasn't appealing. Margaret seemed angry. *What's going on, sis?* She would ponder that for many a night.

***

Joe watched Margaret's face as she toured the house. Her eyes seemed to be covered with a haze, as if she were seeing the dwelling in a different sense of reality. And then it dawned on him. *This one's going to be a "no." Strike-out number twenty-seven.* If this were baseball, it would be a complete no-hitter.

Her words brought him back to here and now. "I don't like the stucco on the ceiling."

The realtor shook his head. "I thought you wanted textured ceilings. At least that's what you said during the last walk-through. Did you change your mind?" He waited a long second before quietly dropping the accusation bomb. "*Again.*" He probably meant to keep it under his breath, but Margaret and Joe both heard it.

The woman faced the agent with a cold stare. *Glad that's not me on the receiving end of that look.* "I do believe I actually did. That is, if it's alright with *you.*"

This was like watching a tennis match. Margaret had just drilled a rocket to the very corner of the backcourt single's sideline. The agent lobbed his volley back just across the net. "I get the feeling you're not happy with my service."

Margaret's return was right down the line and the realtor didn't even have a chance to lunge. "It's simply amazing that you're so perceptive. I think I'll try another agency in the future. Good day, sir." She spun on her heels and grabbed Joe's hand. "I'm ready to go. Come along, please."

Like an obedient puppy, he followed Margaret outside. Joe held her door while she climbed behind the wheel, then trotted around the Land Rover. Once inside, he glanced at the man standing on the porch, the one who'd led them to house after house. *Poor guy.*

"Do you think I was cruel to him?"

That potato was too hot to touch. "I don't know what you mean. If you didn't like a textured ceiling, that's perfectly fine. And where did he get off saying 'again'? I mean, isn't it a girl's prerogative to change her mind?"

She didn't glance in his direction, but he could see the smile in her eyes. "I knew there was a reason I liked you. I'll call him later and apologize. I do believe I'm a tad difficult to put up with these days."

"I don't think that's correct. You're... what's the word I'm looking for..."

"A witch?"

"Never. You see, I was thinking of... *perfect.*"

The corners of her eyes curved as she smiled. "That's because you see me through rose-colored glasses."

*I do, and that's because I'm in love with you.* The vehicle was silent for a moment. "It didn't have anything to do with the ceiling, did it?"

Margaret's smile disappeared. "No."

"What's going on, Maggie?"

He was surprised at the look of sadness on her face. "I'm beginning to think I made a horrendous mistake moving back east. Maybe the reason I keep finding fault in every house we've looked at is because I don't want to be tied down. I want to keep my options open in case I decide to leave."

While he realized she'd just shared some very intimate feelings, his chest ached as he processed her words. The warmth of her hand touching his startled him.

"I know how that sounded, but listen to me. I'm not talking about you. Please understand that. It's my family that's causing the issue. If I hadn't started this vineyard, I believe I'd be gone already. The happy and loving family I remember no longer exists. The world has changed and I'm, I'm having difficulties accepting it."

Her hand still gripped his. "How can I help?"

She squeezed even tighter. "Just be you. I don't think all my years of education can help me find words to explain how I feel about you. You've become my best friend, almost as if we're one. I believe I'd be losing the struggle without you to cling to."

*She just said she cares!* For the rest of his life, Joe would wonder why the following words escaped from his lips. "Forget looking for a house. Move in with me."

Margaret didn't respond right away. He detected a hard swallow and her eyes were shiny. She slid the vehicle to the side of the road, shifted into park and then turned to face him. Her words were slow, as if she were seeing if each one fit. "Joe, if I've led you on, please forgive me. I am not ready for that type of a relationship and all the problems that go with it. The added stress could drive me off the deep end if it didn't work. I've grown accustomed to you being there and I, I need you, but please understand, just not in that way. Sorry if my affection for you was misinterpreted."

He'd been cold-cocked and knocked off his feet before in his life, but that hadn't hurt nearly as bad. *Did I ever read that one wrong? She doesn't love me—yet.* But he couldn't let her down, not with the way he felt about her. And, hope beyond hope, she might someday fall in love with him.

"We're friends, Maggie, close, close friends. You misunderstood. I'm offering to share my home, not my bed. I'm offering as a friend, not as a boyfriend."

The color drained out of her face. "I guess I'm sorry in a different way. Why would you want me to move in with you?"

"Because my friend needs a place to stay, while she decides if she's going to remain in Lancaster... or move on."

Her lips parted as she gauged him. "Suppose I decide to have friends over? Male friends?"

*I'll probably jump off Chickies Rock.* "It would be your place, too. You don't need my permission, as long as whatever you're doing isn't illegal."

A smile now graced that beautiful face. "Okay, no casinos or exceptionally loud music. What are the rules?"

"There are none. Just enjoy yourself and know it's not just my place, it is your home, too."

"How much is the rent?"

*Marry me some day?* "Nothing. Friends don't take advantage of each other." She began to protest. He held his finger to her lips. "If you buy half the food, do your own laundry and don't use all the hot water, I'm good with this."

"And you're sure?"

"Absolutely. Maggie, I'm doing this because I want you to be happy. I think the world of you. And in case you didn't know it... you're my best friend, too."

For the second time in just a few minutes, her actions caught him off guard. Margaret threw her arms around him. Those delicious lips were against his ear. "I'm so happy you're mine... too. Thank you. We'll have a blast, Joe. I promise."

## Chapter Nine

*Three Weeks Later*

Joe didn't even have time to knock before the door swung open and his dear friend Daisy Elliot greeted him with a warm hug. "Hey. It's been a long time since you've stopped by. I was beginning to think you didn't like us anymore. Step inside. Jake and I were working on the baby's room." She turned and directed her voice up the stairs. "Jake, honey? We have a visitor."

"Be right there."

Daisy smiled. "Want to have a seat?"

"Sure." As soon as he'd plopped into the easy chair, Daisy's husband bounded into the room. The man shook his hand. "Hey, Jake."

"Good to see you, Joe. I was beginning to think you'd joined the foreign legion or maybe you'd been abducted by aliens. Want something to drink?"

"Yes, but wait a second." He turned away from Jake. "I, uh, had a couple of hours tonight and I know I've sort of neglected our friendship lately..." He handed a bag to Daisy. "I brought both of you a little something. Open it."

Daisy's white teeth were revealed when she smiled. "You didn't have to." She removed several plastic encased cardboard sheets, then gasped as she showed it to Jake. "Disney characters? Oh, they're so dear. And look at this picture of the castle and the saying... 'Dreams Do Come True'. Are these decals?"

*I did good.* "Um-hmm. My contribution to the nursery."

Daisy reached across to squeeze his hand. "Thank you. This is so unexpected."

"Well, you know, the two of you are awe-inspiring. A shining reminder that true love and happily ever after really does exist in today's world." His gaze returned to Jake. "Brought something special for you, buddy. I can only guess how hard Daisy is making you work. Just reach in there. Take the one on the right."

The other man extracted a bottle of wine. Two labels decorated the container. Margaret's brand banner was at the top. The decal was a circle with the Scottish flag flying above a fair-haired girl who stood overlooking the highlands. Around the periphery, a beautiful script emblazoned the words, 'The Scottish Lass Vineyards of Paradise'. The second marking was a metallic-looking oval with scalloped edges and images of blackberries. The words 'Sweet Evening Dreams' crossed the image.

Jake held it at arm's length. "Wow, blackberry wine... my favorite. This is really cool. Can't wait to taste it." Jake displayed the bottle to Daisy.

Her eyes studied the glass jar before falling on Joe. "This is from Margaret's wine press, isn't it?"

A warmth filled him. "Yes. There's a second bottle in there—alcohol free. She likes to offer the virgin pairing for those who don't like to drink alcohol. She sent it along for you, Daisy, since you're pregnant."

Jake grasped both bottles. "I'll go pour us all a glass. Be right back."

From across the coffee table, Daisy was watching him. "That was nice of her."

"Maggie is a very kind person."

Daisy wrinkled her nose. "Maggie? I thought you said she only liked to be called Margaret."

"She decided her closest circle of friends should call her Maggie from now on." He could sense the question before she spoke. "It isn't just me. Didi and Leslie call her that, too. Oh, I forgot. She's also tight with two of her workers and asked them to use Maggie as well."

"I see. How's the plan going?"

Heat rose from his neck up. "Things are, shall we say, progressing... just a bit."

"Really? How so?"

He studied his friend for her reaction. "She moved in with me."

Daisy's face paled. "You're living together?" Her eyes grew bigger than dinner plates.

Without thinking, his hands moved in front of him as if to defend against negative thoughts. "Platonically. We're sharing the living space, not a bed." He slicked back his hair. "Daze, I'm madly in love with her, but she's, she's just not there. Not yet, but I'm praying with all my heart that someday she will be." He paused to swallow hard. "I took your suggestion. We're developing a deep friendship first." Emotion caught in his throat. "When she said she was considering leaving Lancaster, I, uh well, I had to do something. It was the only thing I could think of. I couldn't risk losing Maggie."

Daisy's hand was warm where she touched him. "Oh Joe, just have faith. Don't push her. We talked about this before. Let her discover the wonderful heart inside you. If you reveal your true self, I wholeheartedly believe things will just fall into place. Allow love to bloom. Remember, God brought you together for a reason."

"I'm trying to be patient, but it's hard. You know, on rainy days, we binge watch television. She loves those miserable zombie shows and no matter where she is seated when we begin watching TV, at the end of the night, she ends up tight against me. Holding hands or clinging to me. And usually, she falls asleep with her head on my shoulder. You have no idea how difficult it is to sit there with the girl of my dreams next to me, and not kiss her."

"It sounds like she trusts you."

"I believe that's true. She told me I'm her best friend. Any suggestions?"

"Persevere, my friend. Run the good race."

*Like you did when you were waiting all those years for Jake?* "I'm trying, I really am."

He touched her arms. "Daisy, be honest. Is there something wrong with me?"

"Absolutely not and stop it. If you keep telling yourself you're not good enough, it will come true. Instead, I want you to repeat after me. I'm going to win her heart and Maggie is going to marry me."

"I wish..."

Daisy threw her hands up in the air. "No! Repeat it. I'm going to win her heart and Maggie is going to marry me."

Joe sighed. "Only for you. I'm going to win her heart and Maggie is going to marry me."

Jake's voice startled him. "That's the spirit, Joe." He handed out champagne flutes filled with a dark purple liquid. "This is ironic. You realize that, don't you?"

Joe was confused. "What do you mean?"

"We're drinking a toast to you winning Margaret's heart... using the wine she made."

Daisy chortled. Joe turned to face her. "What's so funny?"

"What Jake just said... It's all in God's plan." She raised her glass of juice. "Cheers!"

***

Margaret topped off Didi's glass of tea. Her friend's son was chasing one of the season's last fireflies. "LBJ seems to be enjoying himself."

The blonde had a wistful smile. "Ah, to be young and innocent again. I do my best to make his life as happy as possible."

Margaret could sense Didi's sadness. *I need to build her up.* "From what I've seen, you're doing an excellent job. When you went inside a little while ago, your son told me his daddy will soon be coming home."

Didi brushed her cheek. "I try to be positive, even when I start to lose hope."

Margaret took her hand. "Don't you dare go down that path. Next time you start to falter, call me. I'll be there when you can't go on alone."

"Don't get me started."

"Started at what?"

"Let's change the subject, okay?"

Margaret smiled. "What do you want to talk about?"

Didi wiped her cheeks. "I really like this place. The yard looks a lot different than it did that day. Remember? The day you broke his mirror." The blonde girl laughed. "And here we are, a short couple of months later... and you're living here. Who'da thunk it?"

Margaret felt her cheeks heat. "One thing at a time. I helped with the backyard, just a tad. Now, as far as living here..."

Didi's smile was wide. "I wasn't judging. So, what's it like living here?"

"Actually, it's a lot of fun. We seem to have this connection. It doesn't matter what we do. Whether it's cooking, or shopping or even cleaning, it's like... like this is where I'm supposed to be. I know it's only a couple of weeks, but I've never been happier."

"Mommy, Mommy! Look!" LBJ ran to Didi, holding a frog. "Ribbet, Mommy, ribbet!"

Didi was laughing. "Where did you find him?"

Margaret knelt in front of the little boy. "This is Anthony, my friend Joe's favorite frog. He lives in the pond. Can you help me drop him back into the water?"

After depositing the frog in the pond, LBJ went off to chase the illuminating bugs.

Margaret realized Didi had grown silent. "What's on your mind?"

Didi seemed to be studying her glass. "I'm thinking how lucky you are. You're sharing your life with the man you love."

*Love?* "Wait, I never said that."

"Said what, love?"

"Yes. That word never left my lips."

"You don't need to say it, Maggie. It's all over your face. I hope you realize how blessed you are. I'd give everything in the world to have just one more day with Luke."

"How long has it been?"

"Thirty-seven months and eighteen days. That's the day I kissed him goodbye and watched his jet take him off to war." Didi shook her hands as if to dry them. "Enough talk about me. Tell me more about you and Joe."

Margaret watched the first star appear. "He's my rock. In this chaotic world with my weird family, his friendship anchors me. Someone I can depend on... trust to have my back. Did I tell you about the realtor that showed us the last house?"

"No. What happened?"

"I didn't like his attitude, so I was snotty to him, I know I was. But when I asked Joe if he thought I was nasty, do you know what he said?"

Didi turned to look her square in the face. "He sided with you and acted like you'd done nothing wrong, didn't he?"

*How'd she know?* "Well, yes, but how did you guess that?"

"Because Luke would have acted the same way. And that's because he loves me. Why do you think Joe sided with you?"

"I, uh, maybe because he values our friendship?"

"I don't doubt he does. Why else?"

The conversation was suddenly uncomfortable. "Let's talk about something else."

Didi laughed for a few seconds. "It's getting late anyway." She stood and smoothed her shorts. "LBJ? Come say goodbye to Auntie Maggie. We need to go, baby."

"I'm glad you came over. Maybe we can do this again next week?"

Didi had picked up her son. "That would be great. Do me a favor?"

"Sure, what's that?"

"When you invite me over next time, I want to meet him."

Margaret ran her hand through her hair. "You already did meet him."

"Come on, Maggie. Have Joe eat dinner with us."

"Why?"

"I want to meet the man you love. You're my friend, so he'll also be my friend."

"Didi, I'm not in love with him."

"Whatever you say. You can fool yourself, but not me. Face the facts. Maggie Campbell, you're in love with Joseph Rohrer."

## *Chapter Ten*

*Thursday Afternoon*

*J*oe stumbled from his room and then headed for the kitchen. It had been two in the morning when he finally made it home after his shift at the hospital. This morning, the mouth-watering scent of frying bacon and the delectable aroma of Hawaiian coffee were like lover's arms wrapping around him. But it was the sight of Margaret standing behind the counter that made him want to be fully awake. She was sporting those violet-colored shorts and that lacy sleeveless blouse she wore in the mornings before changing to head off to work. And the way her locks cascaded across her shoulders... *exquisite.*

"Morning, sleepyhead. I waited up until midnight for you. What was the lady's name?" She handed him a cup of coffee.

"Thanks, Maggie." He wanted to catch her reaction. "Her name is Contessa." As he watched, Margaret's face paled. Joe continued. "Her husband had a heart attack. She's one of my patients and I sat with her until her daughter drove down from New York. I didn't want her to be alone."

Margaret's eyes glistened as her color returned. "That was sweet of you. You're a compassionate man and I'm proud of you." Her hand found his and she gave it a quick squeeze before returning to the stove. "I made breakfast—bacon and eggs, with home fries. Your favorite, if I recall."

There was a glow about her this morning. "There you are with that photographic memory thing of yours. What did you do last evening?"

"Leslie and I were at the shop until eight, putting on the finishing touches for Saturday. After that, I came home and moped around, missing you. You know, zombie shows aren't nearly as fun to watch when you're not here. I only watch them because they're your favorites." She handed him a plate of steaming food.

"Thank you. Mind if I give thanks this morning?"

"Please do." Her hand again found his and the warmth of her touch made it hard to concentrate.

"Father, we thank You for this food. Please bless it and the hands who prepared it. Also, thanks for the beauty of late August mornings and the strength and comfort of close friends. As You know, Maggie has an important day coming up this week... the opening of her showroom. Please bless her endeavor, but more importantly, please bless my friend with happiness. Amen."

"Amen." They ate in silence for a minute or two before she spoke. "I want you to know, I am happy, for the most part. And your friendship is one of the main reasons." She took another sip of her coffee.

It was so hard not to wrap his arms around her and kiss those beautiful lips. He had to change the subject. "I appreciate your friendship, too." Joe cleared his throat. "Since we're making confessions, I would also like to make one."

Margaret's expression told him he had her full attention. "I'm ready."

"Please don't be offended or take this the wrong way..."

Her eyes studied his. "My mind is open. Just say it."

*Is she afraid I'll tell her there's someone else?* "Okay, here goes." He took her hands in his, noting they were trembling. "I hate to tell you this, but... I hate those zombie shows."

She jumped and stood looking down at him. "What? That's your big confession?"

"Well, yeah. Were you expecting me to say something else?"

She shook her head, but avoided looking directly at him. "Uh, no. So, if the undead aren't your cup of tea, why did you watch them?"

"Duh! Because you like watching them, I adjusted."

She stamped her foot for emphasis. "I hate zombies! Joe, this relationship has to be fair. You need to do a better job communicating, okay?"

*I think she protests too much.* "Yes, ma'am."

"Ma'am is what you call my mother. I'm Maggie... to you. Tell me, sir, what do you like to watch?"

"Sir? That's my dad. My name, in case you forgot, is Joe. And I like musicals."

"Musicals? Why?"

"In high school, I was involved in the musical theater. I played Ali Hakim in *Oklahoma*, Luther Billis in *South Pacific* and Professor Harold Hill in *The Music Man*."

She fought back a giggle. "I'm sorry. I just can't imagine you singing."

"Ha! Oh ye of little faith. I'll have you know I can not only carry a tune, but I can also direct a band." Joe turned to his left and tapped the butter knife as if it were a baton. "Pay attention, River City Boys Band. Let's play Beethoven's *Minuet in G*." Pretending to direct, he started to sing along. "La-di-da-di-da-di-da-di-da...la-di-da, la-di-da."

Margaret could no longer hold it in. A loud guffaw erupted and she doubled over with mirth.

Joe tapped his knife against his plate. "Excuse me, young lady. How about a little respect for a graduate of the Gary Conservatory's Gold Medal class of aught-five?"

She suddenly turned and ran down the hall. "Be right back."

"Where are you going?"

She turned to the left at the end of the hallway. "Bathroom!"

Joe shook his head. "Yep. There's nothing like a dame."

\*\*\*

Margaret was having trouble concentrating. The showroom's opening was a mere two days away. The refrigerators for the sample bottles were loaded. The simple task of filling the wine racks shouldn't have required much attention, but it seemed almost impossible. *What is wrong with me?*

"Miss Campbell? Would you like me to do this for you?"

She turned to find Rebecca Stoltzfus standing next to her. "Please, call me Maggie. I'm not just your employer, you're my friend and hopefully you consider me one of yours."

A smile filled the Amish girl's face. "Yes, we are friends, *Maggie.* Gud friends. Can I finish storing these for you?"

"That would be nice. Thank you."

"Maggie?"

"Yes?"

"When it's just us, I mean Isaac and you and me, could you call me Becky?"

"Of course, *Becky.*"

The girl's expression changed. "Can I ask you a question?"

"Sure."

Before Rebecca could speak, a crashing noise flowed in from the supply room. Both women rushed in to discover Isaac standing in the middle of a mix of debris. Rebecca spoke out. "What happened?"

The man seemed disappointed in himself. "I'm a klutz. I was moving these boxes of wine bottles to the shelf and I guess I clipped the shelf brace with the skid. Whole danged thing came tumbling down. Watch where you step. There's broken glass everywhere." He looked directly at Margaret, "Sorry, boss. I'll pay for what I broke."

"Are you hurt?"

He shook his head. "Only my pride. Can't believe I was this stupid."

"It's okay. It's just things." She surveyed the rack. "Can you do something to the rack to make sure it doesn't happen again?"

"Yes, ma'am."

"Isaac..."

He removed his purple ball cap. "I mean yes, Maggie."

"Do you need a hand fixing this or cleaning up the mess?"

Rebecca quickly volunteered. Margaret returned to the showroom. There was so much to do to finish getting ready. She returned to loading the wine shelves. She contemplated her employees, Isaac and Rebecca. They were a great team, but there was something more about them. They were good friends. Margaret recalled overhearing their conversations. Her mind drifted to Joe. *We're close friends, too.*

The sound of a power tool being used in the storeroom interrupted her thoughts, but only for a second. Joe's face filled her mind. Why had she felt so anxious when he told her he had been with a woman last night... or so relieved to find it was only a patient? She'd felt so shaky when he told her he had a confession to make. And then finding out he had been an actor in high school?

A giggle bubbled up from within her. She found it hard to picture the suave and debonair doctor playing a cowboy or sailor or even a conniving con man. Not him... not her Joe. He was kind... thoughtful... considerate... and so handsome. Joe was a man any woman would be thrilled to have. *Wait! What about me? How do I feel about Joe?*

The words Didi had spoken the other night seemed to well up inside of her. *"Face the facts. Maggie Campbell, you're in love with Joseph Rohrer."*

Margaret stopped loading the rack and instead extracted her cell phone from the pocket of her jeans. The photo on the screen had been taken in the backyard. The garden she'd helped him plant. It was a selfie of the two of them. Joe looked so happy, but that wasn't what drew her attention. Instead, it was the joy in her own face. *How can that be?* Her world was so stressful, with the launch of the business and the letdown by her family...

But she'd missed it, until now. The photo revealed a woman who exuded bliss. And why? *Oh my God!* Could it really be that what Didi said was right?

"Am I really in love with Joe?"

The man's laughter startled her. "I should hope so. Rumor has it that you're living with him." Her brother Henry stood before her. "In sin."

## Chapter Eleven

*7.2 Nanoseconds Later*

*A*nyone within a hundred-mile radius would have to be blind not to see the anger covering Margaret's face. Henry was close enough that he could almost feel the heat coming off of her. His little sister's jaw was clenched as the words spewed from her lips. "Excuse me? What did you say?"

Henry couldn't help himself. He bent over with laughter. "My little Maggot..."

The sharpness of her slap wiped the smile off his face. "You hypocrite. How dare you insult me, in my own place. I wish you weren't my brother. I hate you."

Henry's hand grasped Margaret's wrist before she could backhand him. "Whoa, lass. I was just kidding."

She kicked his shin until he released her arm.

"Margaret! Calm down."

"Calm down? You just accused me of being a—"

Henry stepped forward, wrapping his left arm around her waist while covering her mouth with his right hand. "I didn't mean to offend you, and I was just joking. Ellie and I simply don't understand why you left our home, without so much as a word as to why. What's going on? Did your feelings for Joe make you leave our house and run to him? Are you in love with him? Is that it?"

Margaret reached behind her back and pinched his arm, right where he'd been shot when he rescued Ellie. He quickly released her. *She knows that's my Achilles heel.*

"I am not in love with him! I moved in with him, because... because... if you're so smart, why don't you figure it out? If you were honest, you would know."

"Why in the world are you so angry? What did I do to you?"

Margaret turned and started to walk away.

Henry quickly caught up to her and spun her to face him. "Talk to me. You at least owe me the courtesy of—"

"I don't owe you crap. Get out of my way... *now.*"

When he didn't move, Margaret tried to punch him in the solar plexus, but he had anticipated it. After all, he was the one who'd shown his sister how to defend herself. He caught her arm and gently twisted it behind her back.

She screamed, "Get your hands off of me!"

"As soon as you calm down so we can talk like adults."

"I think you need to release your sister right now, Mr. Campbell."

Henry whipped his head to the source of the words. Both Isaac Golden and Rebecca Stoltzfus were standing there watching him. Rebecca's hand covered her mouth. Isaac's lips were set in a fine white line.

"Mr. Campbell, I think you're hurting your sister and I can't allow that." Isaac stepped closer.

Margaret growled. "So help me... Get your hands off of me, Henry."

"I will, as soon as you act sensibly."

Isaac grabbed Henry's shoulder. "Mr. Campbell, let Maggie go. Please, sir. I won't ask again."

Henry's anger was quickly rising. The harder Margaret struggled, the tighter Henry pulled her against him. *And who is Isaac to tell me what to do?* "Butt out, Golden."

"Henry! You're hurting me."

Isaac made his move as he hissed. "That's it." The man released Henry's shoulder and grabbed Henry by the throat with his left hand while he struck Henry's left arm with his right. Directly on the scar.

The pain was excruciating, forcing Henry to release his sister. Henry pinwheeled his right arm, breaking Isaac's grip. Then he jumped to a defensive position. Isaac took a step backwards and held his hands in front of him. "Whoa, boss. I was just trying to get you to leave her alone."

"How dare you touch me! You're fired. Get off my property right this instant before I decide to throw you off myself."

"No, he's not fired. Isaac, don't go anywhere." Margaret stood a few feet away, hands on her hips. "Henry has no authority in my house."

Before Henry could move, Rebecca shuffled in between him and his sister. "I think it best if you leave Maggie be, Mr. Campbell. Please?"

*What does she think she's doing?* "My sister's name is Margaret. Maggie is my daughter's name. I would appreciate if you'd get that right."

Margaret raised her chin, as if she were looking down on Henry. "My true friends call me Maggie."

Henry whipped around to face her. "True friends? What about your family? Don't you consider us your friends?"

Margaret's face was bright red. "Family? You mean those strangers that replaced the loving people I once knew?"

Henry took a step toward his sister, moving to his left.

Rebecca shifted to block his way.

He eyed the Amish girl. "What are you doing?"

"I-if you want to get to M-Maggie, you'll h-have to go through me first." Her chin was trembling.

Isaac now stood next to the Amish girl. The man's jaw was set and his fists curled. "Correction. You'll have to go through both of us."

Henry stared at the man. "You do realize I'm a former Commando, a Royal Marine, and that I served in the Special Boat Service for her Majesty, don't you?"

"So? I fought for Uncle Sam as a United States Marine. And one thing about us Marines, we don't quit. We never give up. You want to get at your sister? You need to get past me first. If you think you're man enough."

*Insolent, ungrateful...* Henry's face heated and he saw red. "If I wanted to, I could easily..." *No, this isn't the way.* He stopped and shook his head. "This is ludicrous." Henry took a step backwards to diffuse the situation before facing Margaret. "Margaret, believe it or not, I was only joking with you."

"Accusing me of 'living in sin' is your idea of a joke? And to top it off, this coming from you? Ha!"

*I'll ignore the jab.* "The reason I came over was to see if you needed help for your grand opening on Saturday."

She stepped around Rebecca and Isaac. "I have plenty of help, thank you."

"Your other brothers along with Ellie and I want to be here for you and your big day."

"There's no need."

"But we're your family."

Her smile could have lit up the Grand Canyon at night. "Really? How delightful. You mean so you can support me?"

*Finally, she's thinking clearly.* "Absolutely. You know we're all about family. There's nothing more important in the world."

Her smile dissipated. "Really? Then why does my family act as if I don't exist?"

\*\*\*

Joe parked his Camaro next to Maggie's Land Rover. He recognized the other two vehicles sitting in front of the showroom. The old Ford truck belonged to Isaac Golden, but the big black Suburban belonged to the woman who was now Isaac's wife. Leslie, as in Joe's ex-girlfriend. This would be the first time he'd seen her since the breakup. Getting through the night was going to require a heaping helping of courage. If Maggie hadn't asked, he wouldn't be here. His eyes returned to the Suburban.

*I loved you, Leslie.* But he had messed up. Joe hadn't been totally honest with Isaac's wife. And because he'd withheld the truth, Joe ended up as the big loser. Of course, Leslie seemed to have come out all right. She married Isaac just three months after Leslie dumped Joe and, from everything he'd heard, the newlyweds were living in bliss.

A bicycle was leaning against the shop. *Must belong to that Amish girl... what was her name?* "Rebecca. That's it." While Margaret said there were others who helped out, Isaac and Rebecca were his friend's favorites.

Joe lifted the pizza boxes from the passenger seat and headed for the front door. Before he reached it, Rebecca swung the glass open.

"Evening, Mr. Rohrer. I'll take them from you."

"Okay, Rebecca. Please call me Joe."

She didn't turn from him. "You and Maggie are close friends, true?"

At the mention of Margaret's name, Joe's chest warmed. "Yes, we are."

The Amish girl's face reddened. "Then from now on, call me Becky. But just when no one else is around. Is that okay?"

"Yes."

She smiled and then turned away. He followed the girl into the back storeroom. Isaac was dragging in a piece of plywood to the center of the room. Joe nodded at him. "Want some help?"

"That would be nice. I already have wine cases set up as supports, so this sheet will serve as the tabletop."

The two men placed the wood on top. There appeared to be some sort of unspoken communication between the two who worked for Margaret. Without a word, Isaac took the pizza boxes from Rebecca. She grabbed a paper tablecloth, fluffed it like a sheet over the bare wood before draping it over the top and then she quickly set the table with paper plates.

Two women's voices sounded from the showroom. The door swung open and Margaret and Leslie walked in.

A shudder ran down Joe's back as he took in Leslie. Those bright blue eyes seemed to light the room. Leslie quickly kissed Isaac, acknowledged Rebecca and then turned to Joe. Her complexion seemed to pale. She extended her hand. "Good to see you, Joe. You're looking well."

Joe hoped Leslie couldn't pick up the trembling in his hand when they shook. "As do you. Seems marriage agrees with you." He couldn't help but remember the taste of her lips and the warmth of her embrace.

"I'm very happy." Leslie directed her eyes toward Margaret. "Looks like someone else is, too."

Before he could answer, Margaret's arms engulfed him. Her words were whispered. "I missed you so much. It was a horrible day, until you called." For whatever reason, Joe had felt the overwhelming urge to phone Maggie in the middle of the day.

Margaret seemed relieved when she answered the phone. "I don't know how you knew I needed you, but thanks again. You rescued me from my brother."

"I'm glad I could be there for you."

"Like a knight in shining armor." At those words, she pulled away from him, her face beet red.

*Why is she blushing?* He caught the look shared between Leslie and her husband. He read it easily enough. That was Leslie's "I told you so" look.

Rebecca spoke and got everyone's attention. "We should probably eat whilst the food's still warm. We have cheese, vegetable and meat pizzas. I'll serve. What would everyone like?"

Plates were passed around until everyone had at least two slices. Joe found the seating arrangements to be a little peculiar. Leslie parked herself between Rebecca and her husband. Joe was to Rebecca's right. Margaret was seated at the head of the table, between Joe and Isaac. When the last person was seated, Margaret offered her hands and everyone joined in.

The fair-haired lady bowed her head and spoke. "Dear God in Heaven, I want to take a moment to thank You for the blessings around the table tonight. Especially for the gift of true friendship. Of friends closer than any brother or sister I could ever imagine. Thank You again for these many blessings."

When Margaret grew silent, Leslie continued. "And we would be amiss not to give thanks for Margaret and her vision. Please allow her dreams to come true and bless her vineyard with an explosive bounty of blessings."

Isaac now continued. "Father, my friend Maggie has worked hard to achieve her dreams. I think she's a little nervous. Grant her peace and let her know, pass or fail, there's a group of people who will always have her back."

Isaac's voice grew dim. Joe popped open his eyelid to glance at Rebecca. He'd heard Amish men pray before, but Amish women? *I better jump in.* "God? Hi. I know you love it when your children do well. Maggie has worked her heart out to see her vision come to fruition. Please bless her and everything she does." He waited before saying "Amen," because he didn't know if Rebecca would speak. She did.

"Father, you love it best when your children do things that are pleasing in your eyes. Now, making wine can be for evil or for good. I hear so many stories about men, and women, who drink too much of it to be nothing but evil for them. But it can also be pleasing, in moderation. At the wedding in Cana, your Son turned water into wine and that pleased You."

Joe, who was holding the Amish girl's hand, felt her shift. "And I know You read the heart of every man and woman. You keep track of every deed, good and bad. Well, in my eyes, this woman, Maggie Campbell, deserves every blessing you have in store for her. She's a real gud woman, Lord. Bless her with success, yes, but more importantly, bless her with your goodness... and love. She surely follows Your ways, treating people as You do. Please bless my friend Maggie. And, lest we forget, thank You for this food. Amen."

Joe asked a question before he took a bite of the meat pizza. The scent of baked bacon and pepperoni whetted his appetite. "So, what went on this afternoon?" Joe asked.

Leslie shot a curious glance around the table. "Something happened?"

Isaac spoke up. "Not too much. I just got fired, that's all."

Rebecca was snickering. "Until Maggie stepped in. She was quite brave."

Joe turned to Maggie. Her eyes alternated between her two workers. "Speaking of courage, my hat's off to both of you for protecting me."

Leslie caught Joe's eye. He still knew her well enough to be able to read her thoughts. Her expression was asking if he knew what they were talking about. He shrugged.

"Since Joe and I aren't mind readers," Leslie said, "can you let us in on what happened?"

Maggie reached for and firmly gripped Joe's hand. *She's drawing her strength from me.* Over the next ten minutes, she talked about Henry's visit and how tense it had been. When Maggie described how Rebecca and Isaac made a human wall between Henry and Margaret, Joe looked at them with a new respect.

Margaret squeezed his hand tightly before she changed the subject. "I think we can finish up with preparations by noon tomorrow. Here's what I have planned for assignments on Saturday. Isaac, do you mind answering questions and doing tours of the processing equipment?"

"Be my honor to do so, boss."

"Thanks. Becky, do you mind helping with the hayrides?"

"Uh, Maggie, I'm Amish. You know I don't drive tractors. I thought Isaac and I were going to do this, together."

Joe could see the smile Margaret sported. "Sorry, but I need him to be able to explain our equipment. We do have a *special* volunteer filling in, but since he's not an employee, I need you to oversee things, okay?"

Rebecca swallowed hard before nodding. "I will." Joe couldn't miss the wink between Leslie and Margaret. Rebecca apparently didn't miss it either. Her brows furrowed, but she didn't say anything.

Margaret turned to face Joe and Leslie. "I know this is a big request, because of your history, but I need the two of you to do the most important job. Joe and Leslie, I'd like you to man the tasting bar. Together."

## Chapter Twelve

*Saturday Morning*

oe's eyes flew open. A banging, clanging noise emanated from the kitchen. It was either someone slinging pots around in the cooking area or Conestoga Valley High School's indoor drumline had decided to practice in his home. A glance at the clock revealed it was exactly four thirty-seven in the morning. Maggie was either angry or extremely clumsy.

He crept down the hall, smiling as he heard the girl's Scottish voice. "Where in the world does he keep that dratted baking soda?"

Joe had to clamp his hand over his mouth. Margaret had one knee on the counter, her opposite foot hanging mid-air to balance herself as she dug her hand into the top shelf of his spice cabinet.

"Where *is* it?"

"It's behind the cereal in the cabinet to the left of the sink."

Obviously startled, she twisted, lost her balance and fell. Joe lunged across the kitchen and slid on his knees, just in time to catch Margaret before her body could hit the floor.

Her left arm somehow wrapped around his shoulders, Maggie's lips so close he could almost taste the sweetness of them. The world seemed to stop. Those gorgeous green eyes were melting his heart. Joe could wait no longer. He leaned forward to kiss her.

Margaret quickly turned her head and stood, placing her hands on the counter for balance. "Joseph Rohrer! You scared the daylights out of me. I didn't expect you to be awake. Why *are* you up this time of day?"

"I wanted to see if Professor Harold Hill and the River City Boys Band were practicing their halftime show in my kitchen."

"What?"

"You were just a tad noisy."

She looked confused. "Nonsense. I was as quiet as a mouse."

He walked over so they were face to face. He hadn't decided if he should again try to kiss her or not. *I really want to.* "Okay, maybe I'm just a light sleeper. What's going on with you this morning?"

Her nose wrinkled. "I don't understand your question."

Gently brushing her silky hair from her eyes, he smiled. "It's not even five o'clock yet. You've got a busy day ahead. What's cooking?"

"Since you hid the baking soda from me, nothing. Yet."

Joe couldn't help but laugh. "Maggie, that's not what I meant. Why did you get up so early?"

She nibbled her lip and gazed into his eyes. "I couldn't sleep."

"Because of the opening today?"

"Yes," she sighed deeply, "and no."

*Boy, that's confusing.* He waited, but she didn't continue. "Would you like to share?"

"Can we sit and have a serious talk?"

A chill rolled down his spine. *Oh no... What did I do?* "Sure. At the table?"

"Yes. I'll make us a cup of coffee first."

Like water pouring through an open porthole on a sinking ship, dread began to fill his soul. *Wish I would have stayed in bed.* After she'd finished with the Keurig, Maggie added the coconut creamer she loved and brought two mugs to the table.

She swallowed hard before starting. "I want to say this and I need you to listen."

*Maggie's dumping me and we're not even a couple.* "You have my full attention."

"Sometimes when I'm very nervous... and anxious... and, to be honest, scared out of my wits, I lose focus. I'm afraid that's going to happen today."

"In what way?"

Her eyes appeared to water and she looked away briefly. "Joe, I had a really bad dream, a nightmare actually. It was so real and miserably sad."

He offered his hands. She took them and then squeezed tightly. "In my dream, it was today. The opening went well, beyond my wildest dreams. Success went to my head. The launch was better than you could imagine. Critics from three of the top industry magazines came, sampled and raved about my wines in their publications. My stock sold out within the hour, with tens of thousands of dollars in orders. I was invited on talk shows to share my story."

Joe couldn't understand her sadness. "That sounds like a great dream. Why do you think it was a nightmare?"

Margaret wiped her cheek before continuing. "I let all that fame and fortune go to my head. After a year or so, some other vineyard became the darling of the media and everyone forgot all about me. I was utterly alone."

He humphed. "You will never be alone. And I'm not just talking about me. Your staff loves you. Leslie adores you, and don't forget about the TV girl, Didi. You know—"

The firmness of the grasp on his hands intensified. "That's just it. You were all gone. Didi moved away. Rebecca got married. Isaac and Leslie were just, well, different. My family washed their hands of me. But the heartbreak was you."

*Me?* "What did I do?"

"You gave up on me. Oh, you and I spoke, but we may as well have been strangers on an airplane. The magic of our friendship was gone. In getting what I dreamed of, I lost everything I needed."

"Maggie, it won't be like that. I will always be here for you."

Her eyes seemed to bore a hole into his soul. "I want you to know how much I appreciate you. That's why I was up so early. I was going to bake you a cake."

Which was the better feeling? Knowing he hadn't screwed up, or hearing her confession about caring for him? "That's not necessary."

She quickly stood. "Joe, can you hold me?"

*You don't have to ask me twice.* He was barely out of his chair when she wrapped him in her arms.

They snuggled in each other's embrace and she whispered in his ear, "I'm scared."

"Don't be. Everything will be just fine. Your A-team has got your back today... actually, every day. If it seems like you're failing, find me. I'll hold you up when you can't stand on your own."

When she released him, her face was right before him. He couldn't help it. He started to shift his head to reach her mouth. For a second, Margaret tilted hers.

Just before their lips touched, she stiffened and freed herself from his arms. Holding her hands in front of her, she was looking at the floor as she shook her head. "Please don't. That's the last thing I want right now."

*** 

Rebecca turned the bicycle onto the lane leading to the vineyard showroom. Several automobiles were already parked in the back, near the entrance to the bank barn. If she hadn't been lost in thought and taken a longer way here, she would have been on time. And now she was a good twenty minutes late. *My mind kept me from my commitment.* The one she'd made to Maggie. The woman who was more than her employer. Maggie was a gud friend, one Rebecca respected almost as much as she trusted Isaac Golden. Maggie was as dear as a sister to her.

The hay wagon was hitched to one of the old John Deere tractors. Golden bales of straw would serve as seats for the riders. Rebecca leaned her second-hand Schwinn against the building.

Today was warm and would probably end up being downright hot. *What would it feel like to wear shorts for the afternoon instead of this full-length dress?* The English women she saw looked so comfortable with their legs and arms out to take in the warmth of the sun. *Shame on you!* Rebecca addressed the tempting inner voice. "Stop it. Don't let pride and temptation ruin your mind. A gud woman needs a pure heart. Concern yourself with the inside and not the outside. Worry not about the heat today, but your thoughts. Today is Maggie's special day, not yours."

The metal on the glass door was cool from the air conditioning inside. Isaac's wife, Leslie, and Maggie's boyfriend, Joe, were standing behind the counter. Maggie was explaining the different wines to them.

"Amber Fields is a fruit wine made from dandelions. Best tasted at room temperature." Margaret picked up another bottle. "Tropic Breeze is our pineapple wine. Suggest it be served as a chilled dessert wine or used as a base for mixed drinks."

Leslie appeared to be quite attentive. "You also have non-alcoholic versions of all of these?"

The fair-headed lady nodded. "We have both virgin and juice versions of most flavors. The non-alcoholic offerings are sweeter. As far as the juice drinks, they are only lightly or non-sweetened to bring out the full flavor of the fruits."

"If you ask me, I'd rather have peach iced tea." Rebecca turned to face the man who had just whispered those words to her. "What about you, Becky?"

She knew her smile was ear to ear. How this Englishman made her happy inside. "Maybe for you, Isaac. For me, I prefer my grandmother's homemade root beer. On hot days, we place a couple gallon jugs in the spring house. It gets purty cold and soothes your thirst. I'll bring some along for you and the missus sometime."

"We'd like that." He appeared to be about to say something, but instead, he smiled at her.

Rebecca had to look away. Despite accepting the fact that Isaac was in love with and married to Leslie and not her, sometimes Rebecca almost allowed her guard down. Her most treasured memory would always be Isaac's last kiss. The one they shared on the day he rescued her from the Fuhrman brothers. That kiss had sealed their relationship as something deeper than friendship or romance could ever reach. Isaac was her soulmate. It might be a sin, but she held that moment in time deep within her heart.

"Make sure you drink plenty of water today. It's supposed to be a scorcher. Don't want you to dehydrate or have anything happen to you." He looked directly into her eyes. "You know, you're the only one of you I've got."

Rebecca's cheeks heated, so she looked away. "You best be careful too, English."

"I'm not English. I'm an American." Isaac winked at her. This was their inside joke.

"You'll always be English to me."

"See ya later, Becky." He walked off.

Isaac normally dressed in jeans and t-shirts, but today he wore dress pants and a nice button-down shirt. And, as always, he proudly sported a purple ball cap, but this one looked new. Now that she thought about it, Rebecca noted Isaac had even trimmed his beard. Her friend was even more handsome than usual today.

Rebecca's entire body heated when she turned from watching Isaac and that was because Leslie, Isaac's wife, stood before her. Leslie nodded in the direction of her husband. "He's a good man, Rebecca. And I know. Isaac's a very good friend to you."

Her mouth was dry. "We're only friends, you have to believe me."

Leslie nodded and then smiled. "I know. Isaac told me you want him to call you Becky. Is that because you're so close?"

"Mrs. Golden, I swear to you—"

"It's okay. Look, I know we haven't, no, I realize *I* haven't been a good person to you. I'd like to change that and start over. Hopefully, someday maybe you'll even ask *me* to call you Becky as well."

"You... you may now, if it pleases you."

"No, I'd prefer to earn that right." Leslie studied the floor. "I was thinking of you, just now. And I want to tell you how much I admire you."

Dread creeped into Rebecca's mind. This woman knew about the kisses Rebecca had shared with Leslie's husband, before he'd started dating Leslie. "I don't understand, missus."

"Please call me Leslie. Do you see the man over my shoulder?"

"You mean Maggie's boyfriend?"

Leslie giggled. "Thank you. I thought I was the only one who picked up on that. Maggie denies it. Claims they're only friends, but I know him well enough to know he loves her. Do you think your boss loves him back?"

"I'm not too bright when it comes to love."

Leslie studied Rebecca's face. "I think you sell yourself short, but anyway, getting back to what I wanted to say. You're a brave lady. You see, I know you loved Isaac, enough that you were willing to give up your faith for him."

It was horribly warm in the room. "That was before you. Golden and I are just friends now."

Leslie touched Rebecca's hand. "I know that, but I need your advice."

"A-a-advice on what?"

"How did you, no, what did you do inside to change that love to be just friendship?"

"Mrs. Golden..."

"It's Leslie. I realize how strange this conversation seems, but I hope you'll tell me."

Her hand trembled where Isaac's wife still held hers. "I don't understand."

Leslie's smile faded. "That man over there, the one who loves Maggie... before Isaac... he and I were in love. He did something and well, let's say, we parted ways and it wasn't pleasant. And part of me, inside, wants to hold a grudge, to hate him."

"Hate is a strong word."

"Sorry, maybe stay mad at him is a better choice. But our friend Maggie wants him and I to work together today. And that's why I thought of you. If Isaac would have treated me like he acted to you, I never would have spoken to him again. But you took the higher road and now look at the friendship you two have. It amazes me. How did you do that?"

"I asked God to help me forgive him... and forgive myself."

Leslie's eyes seemed to have a sadness to them. "Obviously He answered your prayers. Did it happen right away?"

"It was hard, Missus... I mean, Leslie. I believe when you ask Him for something, you have to believe as if He will do everything by Himself, but work at it as if it will come from you. Only. And somehow, God always seems to meet you somewhere in the middle."

Her words seemed to have coaxed a smile from Leslie. "Isaac was right about you."

"I'm sorry?"

"He always says you are wise beyond your years."

"That I am not. But I th-thank you... Leslie."

The older woman took a deep breath. "Let's change the subject. Rebecca, there's someone Isaac and I want you to meet."

"Who's that?"

Before Leslie could answer, Isaac reappeared. "Hey Becky, Leslie, can you come upstairs for a minute?"

"Of course," Leslie answered. The woman waved her hand, indicating Rebecca should follow. Isaac disappeared through the door at the back of the shop.

*I didn't understand any of that conversation.* Was Isaac's wife trying to be a friend or was this some cruel joke? It wouldn't be the first time an English woman played Rebecca for a fool. She climbed the stairs to the top of the barn. In the distance, Isaac stepped outside. *Isaac wouldn't play a trick on me, would he? Not a mean one... not to me.*

It was now quite warm as she stepped into the sunshine. Isaac was standing next to the John Deere, facing away from her. But something was different about him. Instead of that purple hat, he was wearing a green one. *He's wearing work pants? How did he change so quickly?* She stopped, turning to look at Leslie. The other woman had her hand over her mouth, trying to suppress a laugh.

Rebecca turned to face the man in the green hat. "Isaac?"

A voice to her left answered. "I'm over here, Becky." And there he stood, dressed the same as two minutes ago. She pivoted to face the guy at the tractor. "Then who be that man?"

Her mouth fell open when the male turned to her. Rebecca blinked hard and shook her head. *Am I seeing double?* Directly in front of her stood Isaac... or was it? He was clean shaven, but his face appeared to be the same as her friend's. Then Isaac walked over and threw his arm across the other man's shoulders.

Leslie could no longer hold her mirth and loudly guffawed.

Isaac smiled. "Maggie told you that you'd be working with a volunteer today. Let me introduce you to Abraham, my twin brother."

# Chapter Thirteen

*An Hour Before the Grand Opening*

The butterflies in her stomach threatened to carry Margaret away. She'd never been more nervous in her life. Luckily, she was surrounded by her friends and they gave her strength, especially Joe.

The good doctor stood behind the bar, arranging cups and napkins. Just to his left, Leslie was preparing plates with pyramids of crackers and chocolates. The shortbread crackers were there so the customers could refresh their palates between samples of wines.

As a thank you to the guests for coming, chocolate squares were wrapped in a foil with her logo emblazoned on them. Both treats had been made locally, at Hannah's Bakery. The shop had gone so far as to have a cookie stamp and chocolate molds created so the Scottish Lass Vineyard's logo was imprinted on the sweets. Margaret smiled at the thought of the proprietors, Hannah and Sam Espenshade. The pair had met when they both worked for Campbell Farms. That was before starting their business together. *I hope my winery turns out to be as successful as Hannah's Bakery.*

A brand spanking new Ford Expedition stopped right outside her front door. Margaret recognized it and knew the monstrous vehicle belonged to her sister-in-law, Ellie. Margaret sadly remembered the good times she and Ellie had shared in Ellie's old customized pickup. But just like so many treasured family memories, that too was a thing of the past. *Just lives in my mind now.* Ellie had traded in her beloved SUV for the new family "bus." *Why are they here? I can't handle my family today.*

A light but warm touch on her shoulder interrupted her thoughts. "It will be fine. I hope you know I'll be right with you." Joe was behind her. "Tell me how to help you, Maggie."

She grasped his arm. "I sure didn't need this today." The warmth of his hand and depth of their friendship gave her strength. "Stay by my side, okay?"

He nodded. "Anything for you, Maggie."

The chime on the front door sounded. The two couples walked in. Ellie had her hand in the crook of her husband's arm. It had been several weeks since Maggie had lived with Henry and his family or seen her sister-in-law, but the enormity of Ellie's belly was a surprise. Ever graceful, Ellie smiled, reached for and then hugged Margaret. "Sis, I missed you. How have you been?"

"I've been busy."

Ellie released her and surveyed the showroom. "I can tell. This place is really beautiful, and classy. I'm so proud of you, Margaret." The pregnant lady's dimples came out when she smiled in Joe's direction. "Good to see you again, Dr. Rohrer."

"As it is to see you, Ellie. When are you due?"

"Any day now and let me tell you, I'll be glad when this pregnancy's over. Hopefully I'll finally give Henry the son he's always wanted."

*Sophie already beat you to it.* "Can I get you anything? We have non-alcoholic wine and juice."

"Umm, maybe some pineapple juice?"

Margaret turned to face her brother. "What would you like?"

Henry didn't answer immediately. He smiled and watched her. "I'll have the same as Ellie. This is such an exciting day for you. Pops would be so proud of his little girl. Just like I am."

A lump was rising in her throat. *Why did you have to ruin everything, Henry?* Margaret missed the closeness of her family. "Thanks."

The second couple stepped forward. Sophie Miller's abdomen seemed even larger than Ellie's. "Love what you've done with the place. Who did the interior design?"

It took everything Margaret had not to slap the Italian woman senseless. "Leslie. Leslie Golden. You know, she owns Lapp Interior Design." Margaret nodded in the direction of the tasting bar. "She's over there. Can I get you some juice?"

Sophie didn't answer the question, but instead served one of her own. "Is this what's kept you so busy? I thought once you moved back, I'd see much more of you. Used to have some great times, didn't we?"

*We did, until you and Henry had your fling.* "Times change." Margaret glanced at Henry briefly. "Nothing ever stays the same."

Henry spoke up. "Except the love of family. And your family loves you, Maggot."

*Right.* "Thanks for coming, but I've got a lot to do." She knew Joe was right by her side. "Joe, would you mind getting drinks for them? I need to tend to something in the back."

"Of course, Maggie. Everyone, let's step over here. Leslie will serve you."

Margaret walked into the back room and found a place to sit. Less than thirty seconds later, Joe found her. "How are you holding up?"

She reached for him and allowed his presence to comfort her. "Why did they have to come here, today of all days?"

"I believe they just wanted to be here to support you."

"As far as I'm concerned, they should have stayed on their side of the farm." Joe released her and she sat back down, facing him. "That witch has the gall to stand there, right next to Henry's wife and act like nothing is going on. I'd bet a million dollars that child Sophie's carrying was fathered by my brother."

Joe softly touched her face. "Can you do anything about it?"

"Of course not, but—"

"I don't mean to be harsh, but if you can't change the situation, then let it go. Otherwise, you're just torturing yourself."

*Let it go?* Her entire body was now on fire. "What did you say?"

The apparent compassion in Joe's eyes inflamed her even more. "For your own sanity, leave it be." He reached for her hands and held them firmly. "Focus on the things you *can* control and accept there are things that you have no influence over."

"But what my brother is doing is wrong. And no one can tell me Ellie doesn't know."

"Can I make an observation?"

"And what would that be?"

"Henry and Ellie seem happy. Your sister-in-law has a glow and it isn't just the pregnancy. Even I can tell she's in love with Henry. And I believe Henry loves her just as much."

*Henry is cheating on Ellie.* "But the way he and Sophie act—"

"Is beyond your control and, unfortunately, none of *your* business."

She pulled her hands from his grip and shoved him away. *Et tu, Brute? Don't you dare tell me what to think.* "I thought you supported me."

His laugh bothered her. "I do, but don't let them steal your happiness. It isn't worth it. Think happy thoughts. Today is a once-in-a-lifetime day for you. Enjoy it." He stopped and looked directly into her eyes. "You have a choice of what memories you'll keep. You can either be bitter because your family came to support you or else cherish the joy of a successful opening."

She stared at Joe for a while before standing and looking down on him. "I believe the thing I'll remember most is how the man I thought was my best friend betrayed me." Margaret slammed the door behind her for emphasis.

\*\*\*

Leslie noticed the look on Joe's face. *Devastation.* She'd seen it twice before. Once when Aubrey broke up with him and the second time at last Thanksgiving. When Leslie dumped him. Of course, he'd deserved it. Joe had misled her and Leslie was more than justified to send him packing. But seeing the hurt in his eyes made her sad. *I loved him once and hate to see him miserable.* His current expression probably had something to do with the way Margaret slammed the door when she exited the storeroom earlier.

"Are you okay?"

"Just peachy."

"Did you and Maggie have a disagreement?"

He whipped his head around to engage her eyes. "Don't act like you care, Leslie. It's bad enough I'm stuck here with you. I don't need you trying to stick your nose in my business."

*Ooh. Struck a nerve.* "It's no vacation having to put up with you either, let alone your insolence."

Joe clenched his teeth. "We're both doing this for her, so can you try to act civil?"

"Fine, but remember civility takes two." Silence followed until a white SUV from the Harrisburg news station pulled into the lot. A beautiful blonde climbed out.

Leslie touched his arm. "There's Didi Phillips-Zinn. Maggie told me the station was covering the opening, but I didn't think they'd allow Didi to report on it because of her friendship with Maggie."

"You're right."

Leslie almost laughed as she turned to Joe. He smirked. "I know... mark this day down in history. Joseph Rohrer actually admitted Leslie was right."

"Took you long enough."

"Even a blind squirrel eventually finds a nut."

They were quiet as they watched Didi and her camerawoman enter the shop. Didi walked right over to the counter, a wide smile on her face. "Hey, guys! Good to see you again. Where can I find the woman of the hour?"

When Leslie shrugged, Didi faced Joe. "Don't ask me. It's not my day to watch her."

The newscaster looked at him with curiosity. "Are you okay?"

Joe rolled his eyes. "Why is it every woman thinks there's something wrong with me?"

Leslie had trouble keeping the laughter inside. "How much film do you have on that camera? Covering what's wrong with Joe Rohrer would be a full-length documentary."

Didi again smiled and shook her head. The glass door opened and Margaret strolled in. "There she is."

Leslie noticed that Margaret didn't make eye contact with Joe. The Scottish woman embraced the blonde reporter. "Thank you for being here. Where do you want to start? Will someone put makeup on me before you film?"

The laughter of the newscaster filled the store. "Makeup? Of course not. As if you needed that."

While the smile never left her face, Didi explained the plan. "I think I'll interview you in the garden out front. Afterwards, you can lead the camera on a tour and explain how you got started. And why. You know, Maggie's story, told in first person. Afterwards, we'll just film some of the activities and maybe interview a few patrons."

Leslie picked up the tremble in Margaret's hands. So anxious. *Why doesn't Joe go comfort her?* From what her friend told her, Margaret drew much of her strength from the good doctor. Glancing at the man standing next to her behind the bar puzzled her even more. He was wiping down the counter as if Didi and Margaret didn't exist.

Margaret's voice ended her thoughts. "Do you think anyone will come?"

Didi laughed and pointed out of the window. "See for yourself."

All eyes took in the scene. In the ten minutes since the news crew had arrived, the parking lot had filled up.

Margaret's jaw dropped in disbelief. "Wow. This is really happening, isn't it?"

Didi patted her shoulder. "Yes, and we better hurry. I think it's going to be a very busy day for you."

Before she left, Margaret turned to face Leslie and Joe. "Thanks for helping today. I, uh… see you later."

Leslie couldn't contain her giggle. "Good luck. Break a leg."

Margaret shot her a smile, but then her expression darkened when she turned to Joe. The icy beams Margaret directed at him might have killed a mere mortal. The fair-haired girl shook her head and turned to follow Didi.

A glance at Joe revealed sadness and despair. "What in heaven's name did you do, Joe?"

His head slowly shook. "Nothing. This is what I get for trying to be nice."

"Come again?"

"You're looking at the world's biggest loser. A man every woman can hate."

"What's going on between the two of you? Everyone can see you love Maggie and she—"

The firmness of his voice really got her attention. "Stop. This is off limits, especially to you. Either change the subject or serve the customers yourself. I'm about done."

*Wow. Must have been a bad fight.* "Okay. Changing the subject... have you seen the news about the super-storm bearing down on the Philippines?"

He nodded. "Yeah. They're calling it the storm of the millennium."

"I heard one of the weathermen refer to it as a super-typhoon. He attributed it to global warming."

Joe grimaced. "Those poor people. I read the islands are bracing for tsunami-like waves as part of the storm system."

"I'm glad we're not there." The glass door opened and several guests entered. A middle-aged couple approached, looking thirsty. A steady flow of people was right behind them.

Joe whispered, "Brace yourself. Here comes our first wave."

# Chapter Fourteen

*Mid-Afternoon*

*J*oe's legs ached and he was glad it was finally slowing down. The last four hours had been a blur. If he never again breathed in the sweet scent of wine, that would be fine with him. Joe couldn't believe how many people had come out for the grand opening. Close to a dozen cases of empty bottles were stacked behind the tasting counter. Joe was inserting a few containers of white wine into the chilling fridge when he heard a voice from the past.

"Joe? Is that you?"

*Oh no.* He immediately recognized not just the voice, but the happy face of the girl standing on the other side of the counter. He swallowed hard. "Hello, Tara. How are you?"

She was even more beautiful than he remembered. Joe hadn't seen her in almost three years. Their eyes met and everything faded away. And once again, it was the year of his thirtieth birthday. Joe had fallen in love with Tara two years before that, but she'd been in a long-term relationship. He remembered well the day when she'd stopped by his house. It was right after he'd transferred to a new office, so he wouldn't have to face the girl he loved, but would never have.

Joe had opened the door to find Tara Miller on his doorstep. *"Tara? This is a surprise. Come in."*

She'd sat across from him in the living room. It took her no time at all to come to the point. *"That last day you were in the office, you kissed me."* He had, but not intentionally. He'd only meant to say goodbye... to the girl he loved... the one engaged to another man. And when he started to tell her he was leaving, Joe lost control and drew her into his arms. The warmth and wonder of that kiss would stay with him forever. *"Do you remember?"*

*"Yes. I'm sorry. You're in love with someone else and that was wrong of me."*

*"W-why did you kiss me?"*

*"Look, I never meant to slip up like that. It was very unprofessional, I know."*

Tara had moved until she sat next to him on the sofa. *"I'd like to know your intentions. I've felt like there's been something between us for a while. Not out in the open, but beneath the surface. When you kissed me, it was like... like... almost how I imagined the first kiss would be after getting married. As if... as if it were a happily ever after kiss. Let me ask this plainly. That kiss... It felt like you were in love with me. Did I read you right?"*

Answering Tara's question truthfully was perhaps the hardest thing he'd ever done. *"Yes. I fell in love with you when we first met, but I tried never to let it show."*

*"Do you still feel the same way?"*

*"I don't think anything will ever change the way I feel about you."*

He had not been prepared for the warmth of her embrace. Or what she told him. *"Joe, I called off the wedding. I need to know... is there still a chance for us?"* And in that moment in time, there had been. The next three months were the happiest of his life. Other than work, they spent every single second of every day together. But even then, he slowly came to the conclusion that any chance of forever was doomed... because of the other man... the one she'd left. Tara never got over him. Joe had set her free so she could sort out her feelings... hoping she would return...

"So, which wine do you suggest?" The question interrupted the trip down memory lane. The man who was speaking to him *was* the other man. Edmund Campbell, Maggie's youngest brother, was now Tara's husband and the father of her three children.

Leslie touched his arm. "Joe, could you go in the back and get a couple of bottles of white wine? We're running low. I'll take care of the customers."

He glanced at the cooler. There were at least a half dozen bottles of that particular wine in the chiller. *Leslie just bailed me out.* "Good idea." He turned to Tara and Edmund. "Nice to see you again, but you know how it is. Duty calls."

As he walked to the storeroom, he glanced at Margaret. Didi Phillips-Zinn and her camerawoman had departed about an hour ago, but you wouldn't know it from the crowd surrounding her. It was more as if she were a hot pop star than a vigneron. When she glanced in his direction, their eyes met. The smile faded from her lips and she quickly turned away.

*This day stinks.* It was bad enough getting stuck serving samples with his most recent ex, but then to look up and discover Tara in front of him? *What's the probability that two of my three ex-girlfriends would show up here, today?* But that was nothing compared to having Margaret angry with him. *I was only trying to help her.* It seemed she was causing herself undue stress, so he'd offered a solution. *If you can't control it, let it be.* But she was convinced Joe had betrayed her. Nothing was further from the truth. He'd rather die than be disloyal to her.

Joe stopped just inside the storeroom door and petitioned to Heaven, "What could I have done differently?" A voice inside him answered. *Should have kept your big mouth shut.* The nagging feeling of gloom was starting to fill the pit of his stomach... or was it bile? *This is going to end up just like the three other times.* Only this time, the girl didn't even love him. It had been all in his mind. Now was the time to start backing away, to prevent further hurt to himself, or Maggie. *I shouldn't call her Maggie anymore. That name was reserved for her* close *friends.* He ran his hand through his hair. *This pain is worse than the last three breakups all put together.*

It was getting late. He should get back to his station. The shop would close in less than an hour. Joe grabbed a couple bottles of wine and headed back through the door into the store. His feet stopped moving as if they were steel and the floor was a magnet. Standing at the tasting counter stood Leslie's brother... Connor Lapp, the man who used to be his best friend. And right next to him stood the gorgeous, curly-haired beauty that Joe had once loved—Aubrey. His third ex-girlfriend. *Can today get any worse?*

*** 

The sweet, smooth apricot wine tickled her mouth just before she swallowed. The lady standing in front of her represented a national wine and liquor distribution company. The woman's reaction to the tasty beverage seemed quite positive.

"Ms. Campbell, I can honestly say I've never sampled wine as tasty as this. What is that spice I detect?"

Margaret couldn't hide her smile. "That's my private trade secret. It creates the allure of the drink."

Laughter. "Okay, I get it." The other woman's expression changed. "I'd like to pick up your brand. The unique flavors and intrigue of your wines carry quite a potential. You know, I was thinking... would you be able to offer your brand in smaller bottles? I'm thinking both single-serving and miniatures, you know, like the size you get on a flight?"

*We'd have to tool up for that.* "I don't know. I'd need to invest in a different bottling line, redesign the labels and order new packaging material. I'm not sure I could do that right now, just starting up, I mean."

The woman's smile was kind. "And if I offered a three-year contract, with a commitment for, say, twelve thousand a year of each? Would that make it more appealing?"

Margaret felt giddy. *Is it the wine or because my dreams are coming true?* "I believe that might make it worthy of consideration. How about we set up a time to discuss your offer?"

"Perfect. Can we pick a date and time while I'm here? I'd like to bring my sales team along for a tour and tasting experience. Would that be possible?"

"I think we might be able to make that work." Margaret pulled out her phone so she could suggest a date. A chilling sensation started in her shoulders and worked down her arms. The picture on the screen was the selfie of her and Joe... in front of the daylilies they planted together in his backyard.

*Did I overreact?* He hadn't really betrayed her, had he? The whole time she'd known Joe, he'd always been focused on her and helping out. Look at today. Working next to his ex-girlfriend just because she needed him. So selfless. *My best friend and yet, I let my anxiety get the better of me.* Allowing her family frustrations and fear of the unknown to concentrate into a single point of focus. And like a laser beam, he'd been the recipient. She'd taken it out on him.

"Tuesday would work for my team."

*What? Oh, business, that's right.* "Sorry, I got distracted. How about ten?"

"That's perfect. We'll be here. Goodbye."

"Thanks for coming."

After the lady left, Margaret again turned her attention to the sampling bar. Well, to be perfectly specific, to the man standing behind the counter. He was so adorable as he poured out a sample for a middle-aged woman. It was as if time slowed down. Her mind went back to the magic of earlier that morning. The scent of fresh baked cake came flowing back, but that wasn't what had her attention. It was the closeness of his lips. Twice this morning, they'd been close enough to taste. Needing to keep her head clear and mind focused, she'd put aside the real question in her mind. *Joe's my best friend. Do I love him?*

Two teenagers walked in front of her. They each were drinking from her "Green Label" bottles. The green labels signified the product as juice, not wine.

Her eyes drifted back to the doctor. His attention was focused on the polished wood surface in front of him. Margaret's mind wandered again... to Joe, and his kindness. If she was truthful, he'd never tried to hide his affection from her. He wore it on his sleeve like a medal. Joe was her confidant, her playmate, partner in crime, her rock... *and my heart's desire?* If she was totally honest, he had been for years. The voice inside her answered. It was time to go make up.

Before Margaret could walk over, another woman approached the counter. It wasn't as loud as it had been earlier, and Margaret could easily hear the woman's words. But it wasn't so much the conversation as it was the look on Joe's face.

"Dr. Rohrer, what are you doing here? They've got you serving up samples? How have you been?"

*Why is he smiling at her that way?* She wasn't much to look at, well, except the blonde shoulder-length hair that framed blue eyes, red lips and a prettier than average face. Not to mention the woman's figure. *Still…*

His eyes shifted momentarily from the woman to Margaret. There was an emptiness in his gaze, but something struck her. In his eyes, it was quite evident. Pain. *It's because of how I treated him.* Joe winced before putting on a smile and turning back to the lady standing before him. His voice was loud enough to be heard almost everywhere in the shop.

"Hi, Georgia. You look wonderful this afternoon. I know I was distracted during our date, but…"

Margaret swallowed hard. *They dated?*

"I was wondering if, maybe, uh, you'd like to go out to dinner tonight."

The girl was all smiles. "Are you sure you don't have plans for the evening?"

A smile might have been on his lips, but Margaret knew him well enough to know it was forced. "I did, but things change. I'm completely free tonight… now."

\*\*\*

Leslie had been doing her best not to appear to be eavesdropping. *I mean, if you don't have to strain to hear it, it's just listening, right?* She'd felt sorry for Joe. Their broken relationship was still fresh enough in Leslie's mind that she still remembered a lot, like Joe's romantic past.

A customer requested a sample of elderberry wine. Leslie poured it with a smile. If Margaret hadn't asked Joe to do it, there was no way he'd have spent all afternoon sharing counterspace with Leslie. As if that weren't torture enough for poor Joe, Tara had shown up. Leslie intervened and sent him to the back room to get more wine. But just before he returned, Aubrey and Connor, Leslie's sister-in-law and brother, arrived. Another failed romance from the doctor's past.

Leslie studied her pouring partner. Usually, the man couldn't keep his eyes off Margaret, but not so much this afternoon. Leslie suspected the pair had quarreled earlier, based on Joe's foul mood. Time was winding down for the open house, and Leslie felt it was her responsibility to do something to bring them close again.

Then, the blonde bombshell walked in, her eyes on Joe. Leslie did her best to intercept. "Good afternoon and welcome to the Scottish Lass Vineyards. Would you care for a sample of our wines?"

After a diminutive glance in Leslie's direction, she addressed the man who was helping her. "Dr. Rohrer, what are you doing here?"

That was when Leslie noticed Margaret standing maybe ten feet away, just watching Joe and the woman. Her mouth fell open when he asked the girl for a date. Leslie's own head whipped around to stare in disbelief. *What is he doing? Doesn't he see how Maggie cares for him?*

"May I have some of the peach wine... uh, change that. Make it the apricot one, please." The man standing in front of her was about fifteen years

Leslie's senior. He winked when she looked at him. Leslie needed to get rid of him... quickly.

"Here you go."

"What about you? Which one of these flavors do you like the best?"

"White."

"Why do you like that flavor?"

*Give me a break.* "It's my husband's favorite."

"Really? What's your husband do?"

*Time to get rid of him.* "I'm not really sure. He works for some obscure government agency. I think he's a spy or an assassin, really. All I know is he keeps telling me if anyone ever bothers me to tell him and he'll eighty-six them. Not sure what that means. Might have something to do with all those medals he got while in the Marine Corps. Now, if you'll excuse me..."

The man's presence was preventing her from hearing what was going on with Joe and the other woman, apparently named Georgia from what Leslie had just heard. She caught a snippet of Joe's conversation. "I'm just helping out a friend."

The blonde smiled at him. "What were you thinking of doing tonight?"

The man's interruption prevented Leslie from catching Joe's response. "I'd like to try one of the red wines. Which do you suggest?"

She quickly poured from the closest bottle. "Try this one. It's called the Rose of Paradise."

"Is your husband here with you? I've read quite a few spy novels and I'm really intrigued. I'd love to meet him."

"He left for Africa this morning. Now if you'll—"

"Wait. Can I try—"

"Nope. This close to closing, we're cutting guests off at two samples. Thanks for coming by and have a great day."

"Oh, okay. Thanks."

With that customer gone, Leslie could finally give her full attention to what was happening next to her. The blonde smiled and spoke to Joe. "I guess that settles it then. I'll keep an eye out for you and see you at seven. Thanks, Joe. Looking forward to it."

"Can't wait to see you."

Leslie watched in disbelief as the woman walked right to Margaret. "Excuse me. Do you work here?"

"Yes. You could say that."

"I'm looking for a nice dessert wine for later this evening. You know, an after-dinner pairing. I'm confident tonight will be a very romantic evening."

A vacant expression covered Maggie's face. "I see. Come with me and I'll explain what we've got." The two moved away from the tasting bar.

Leslie whipped around to face her drink pouring partner. She kept her voice low. "Joseph Rohrer, what is wrong with you?"

He turned his head so he wasn't facing her and then sighed. "And what did I do now?"

"Why did you ask that woman out?"

"My life and any decisions I make are no longer any concern of yours."

Leslie moved closer, until their faces were almost touching. "It is when it involves a close friend of mine. I don't want to see Maggie get hurt because you're acting like a spoiled little boy."

Her words did the trick. Joe pivoted and faced her. "You can't hurt someone if they don't really care."

"What? Are you insane? Maggie loves you. Can't you see it?"

His face was now red. "Quit sticking your nose in my business. You gave up any right to have any input into my life when you broke up with me."

"Thank you both for coming today." Joe and Leslie paused their conversation and looked up to find Margaret standing there. "It was a good turnout, don't you think?"

Her friend suddenly looked spent. "I do believe it was a success. Congratulations."

Margaret now studied Joe's face. "How do you think it went?"

"I believe your business is off to a great start. I'm happy for you."

"I want you to know how much I appreciate you being here today. It meant a lot to me, Joe."

The man looked away. "No problem. People are supposed to help each other."

"I was planning on taking everyone out to dinner. My treat as a way of saying thank you. I really want you to come, Joe. To celebrate with me. Will you join us?"

His face was now dark red. "I have other plans."

Leslie's heart went out to Margaret. She could see the disappointment in her friend's eyes.

"I see. Wasn't it just this morning that you promised to prop me up when I failed?"

He took a deep breath through his nose before removing the apron he'd worn and dropped it on the bar. He walked out from behind the counter. "But you didn't fail. Today was the success you hoped for. And it couldn't happen to a nicer person."

"Then come celebrate with us, with me."

Shaking his head, Joe looked away. "I don't think that's a good idea, Margaret."

"Margaret? What happened to calling me Maggie?"

From Leslie's view, she caught the anger in his eyes. "You once said you wanted your close friends to call you Maggie, did you not?"

"Yes, I did and I want you to—"

"Then I don't think it's right for me to call you that anymore."

She touched his arm. "Joe, I don't understand."

He pulled away. "People who betray you aren't considered to be close friends, now are they, *Margaret*?"

*Chapter Fifteen*

*Sunday Evening*

*M*argaret threw another piece of wood into the outdoor fire pit. Summer was moving on and the evenings were cooler. The scent of burning wood took her back to a simpler time, when her family lived in Scotland. She'd barely been ten when her mum taught her how to cook on the hearth. Slow roasted lamb stew, hearty beef and kidney pie, and mutton skewers had all been a part of her youth. Being so far removed from the neighbors had meant you learned to depend on family. And the Campbells had been extremely close, even after Henry joined the Royal Marines. The eldest of the Campbell children, Henry had been stationed in nearby Clyde, so he'd visited home quite often.

In the distance of the gathering dusk, a rogue firework rocket probed the night sky. Until he entered the service, Henry had been her favorite brother. He'd always watched out for her. But all that changed when Harry had stepped up to take her eldest brother's place after Henry decided to serve Her Majesty.

Margaret developed an extremely close bond with Harry and for years was the only person in the entire world to know her middle brother's hush-hush confidence. Harry wrote children's books. The two had closely safeguarded the secret until Ashley, the woman who was now his wife, came along. With Ashley by his side, Harry had finally been brave enough to share his books with the world.

A thumping beat, at first barely detectable, grew and grew until the deep bass notes seemed to vibrate Margaret's bones. *How enjoyable could it be for anyone to listen to music that loud?* After the car drove by, the sound disappeared.

The youngest brother, Edmund, was only two years older than Margaret. He hadn't seemed to fit in anywhere in the family. Margaret suspected it was because Pops had died when Edmund was just seven. Margaret had her mum to lean on, but Edmund didn't seem to have, want or need anybody. His wild streak and desire to always get the best of Harry were his trademarks. Only after the fiasco that resulted in Harry intentionally breaking Edmund's arm several years ago had she and Edmund become close, and then only for a brief while.

The quarter moon was slowly rising in the sky. A vision of her family from long-ago days floated before her eyes. Her world had been very comfortable and happy. And now? Those brothers and their families might as well be total strangers.

In the sky, flashing lights were barely discernable above her head. The flight path took the airliner in a southwesterly direction. *Wish I was on that plane. Anywhere but here would be good.* She watched until the beacons faded into the horizon. Margaret's mind drifted to the man who was probably the most important person of her entire life. *Until yesterday.*

From the first time she met him, eons ago when he'd briefly dated her neighbor, Tara Miller, Joseph had inhabited a special place in her heart. She'd seen him intermittently over the years before moving home. And the secret fantasy that lived in her heart had always been of a romance developing between the two of them. But, like her mum always said, anything worth doing has to be done right. Therefore, Margaret had waited until there was sufficient time so she could focus her attention on a real relationship. *As soon as the Grand Opening was over, I'll make the time.* That was what she'd told herself.

The fire needed another log, so she threw one on. Embers rose up into the night before quickly flaring out. *Handling stress has never been one of my strengths.* And then when her brother Henry brought both his wife *and* the woman with whom he was having a fling to the vineyard, it was just too much. Poor Joe had stepped in and tried to help. *I realize that now.* But her frustration had boiled over and she let her best friend have it. *I accused Joe of betraying me.*

The trees on the neighbor's property suddenly illuminated. That meant someone had turned into the drive.

Margaret tried to imagine how difficult yesterday must have been for Joe. First, working with Leslie. *He only did that for me.* After Joe left, Margaret discovered that poor Joe had come face-to-face with his other two ex-girlfriends. Then, top it with how Margaret had blown up in his face? No wonder he'd asked the blonde woman out. That was excusable. *But what he did afterwards was reprehensible.*

Soft footfalls fell behind her. She didn't bother to turn around. "Good evening, Joseph."

He walked until he stood next to her. "Margaret, I need to talk to you."

Her gaze was on the flames. "Do you think that words could possibly make any difference?"

"I hope so. I really screwed up this time."

Margaret took a sip of her wine, still not looking at Joe. "Well, that's one thing we both agree on."

"Maggie, I didn't mean to—"

She held her hand up. When he stopped, she stood and moved until they were face to face. "How was your date last night?"

Even in the dusk, she could see his jaw clench. "When you moved here, you asked about how I'd react if you dated a man. But you're upset because I asked another woman for a date? This seems like a double standard. Maggie, that's not fair."

"Did you ever think I was testing you? I had no intention of dating any man other than you." His expression was one of confusion. "And by the way? You failed the test, miserably."

"But Maggie—"

"And don't call me Maggie, anymore. Going out on a date for revenge, I could understand. But your betrayal... I can't forgive that."

"I'm sorry I tried to help you deal with your family."

"Oh, that part. I apologize for becoming angry for you trying to help. My mistake."

"Then why do you feel I betrayed you?"

"Because you spent the night with her. That's why." Margaret left him standing there, all alone in the dark Pennsylvania dusk.

\*\*\*

Daisy set down her computer bag. The staff, which had been milling around the nurse's station, looked in her direction but ignored her. That changed when the Clinical Nurse Coordinator walked out of his office and loudly cleared his throat. The nurses all scattered. He glanced in her direction and winked. "That's the way it's done, Daze." Trenton returned to his office.

She was just taking a sip of her coffee when a voice grabbed her attention. "Mrs. Elliot, could I speak to you in my office?"

Daisy turned to find Dr. Rohrer behind her. He looked absolutely horrible this morning. "Are you okay?"

He nodded in the direction of his door. "This is personal. Let's talk in there."

Joe entered and Daisy followed. Without waiting for him to motion, she closed the door. "What's wrong?"

He ran his fingers through his hair. "I wanted to thank you and Jake for letting me stay at your place Saturday night."

"You're welcome any time, Joe." Daisy hesitated. "Did you talk to Maggie last night?"

"Uh, yeah. She told me not to call her that anymore. It's Margaret now."

The despair on his face saddened Daisy. "Why would she say that?"

"She thinks I slept with Georgia. The ultimate betrayal, from Margaret's point of view."

"But you didn't. Did you tell her that?"

Joe now gazed out the window. "It's too late. You know, I'm the stupidest man alive. With my luck with women... and this time, I was idiotic enough to invite her to move into my house."

She touched his shoulder. "You need to talk to her, to explain everything. When you tell Maggie the truth, she'll understand."

"That will never happen."

"What? Why? What are you going to do?"

Joe took a ragged breath. "Like you always say, God has a plan. And last night, He revealed to me the path He wants me to take. My days here in Lancaster are over."

"You're talking foolishly. What is that supposed to mean?"

The man sat in his chair and turned to the back table. Picking up a framed photo, he gently ran his finger over the images. It was a photo of Daisy and her husband. "In my life, you've been my truest friend. The biggest regret I'll have will be not being here to see you and Jake raise your kids."

Her shoulders chilled. "What do you mean, you won't be here?"

"You heard about the storm ravaging the Philippines?"

"Y-yes. I heard something on the news that the Navy was considering sending a hospital ship."

"Actually, they're sending in both the Mercy and the Comfort and not one, but two carrier groups." *Are they expecting a war?* He must have read the question in her eyes. "The carriers can provide lots of assets to aid for disaster relief."

"How would you know about that?"

"I got a call last night. Remember that international group I volunteered with two years ago?"

"I think so. You went to Africa for three months, right?"

"Yep. They're pairing with the Navy. Gearing up for a humanitarian mission to the islands. I was asked if I would go. I said yes."

She felt the blood drain from her face. "How long will you be gone?"

Joe sighed. "After the mission, I'm not planning on returning. I'm thinking Hawaii might be a good choice to start over."

"Hawaii? That's six thousand miles away. You are not being rational. This is all a reaction to your argument with Maggie."

"*Au contraire.* That call made me realize I need a change. And that's why I wanted to talk to you."

"Joe, you're not making sense. Okay, I understand your desire to help others, but this is your home. Why would you want to move to Hawaii?"

"Because it's six thousand miles away. I've had enough of life here. Everywhere I look, all I see are my failures."

"Joe, slow down for a minute."

"I'm putting you in charge of my affairs."

*What is wrong with him?* "What affairs?"

"Selling my house, my car and everything else I own."

"This isn't like you. You need to take a deep breath and consider what you're saying."

He removed his ID badge and tossed it on the desk. "Too late."

"What do you mean it's 'too late'?"

Joe stood and walked until he was in front of her. He offered his hand and embraced Daisy after she stood. "This is goodbye. I turned in my resignation this morning." Joe pressed his car keys into her palm. "My Uber is waiting outside. I have a flight that leaves in two hours." He bit his lip and fought off a sob. "Saying this is the hardest thing I've ever done."

"What are you talking about?"

"This is the last time you'll ever see me. Goodbye, Daisy."

She watched in disbelief as Joe Rohrer opened the door and walked out of her life.

# Chapter Sixteen

*Tuesday Morning*

**R**ebecca Stoltzfus was concerned about Margaret Campbell. Her boss had appeared confused and listless yesterday and didn't even respond when Rebecca tried to talk to her. Rebecca needed advice and didn't know whom else to speak with. She was stacking cases of cherry wine when the door from the store opened. Margaret scanned the room, but stopped when she caught sight of Rebecca.

"There you are. Becky, can you step into my office for a few minutes? We need to chat." She didn't wait for Rebecca to follow.

*Did I do something wrong?* Rebecca's arms trembled. This probably had something to do with Saturday and what happened on the hay wagon. Swallowing and gathering her courage, Rebecca stepped through the door and walked until she stood at the entrance of her boss's office.

Margaret was shuffling through some paperwork on her desk and didn't look up when Rebecca entered. "You wanted to see me?"

The fair-haired lady glanced up and her expression seemed confused. The woman then shook her head before nodding at a chair. "Yeah. Please close the door and have a seat."

Margaret's formality caused Rebecca's breathing rate to increase. "Are you angry with me? If this is about Saturday, I can explain. Please don't be cross at me."

Snapping her head to attention, Margaret stared at her. "Why would I be upset with you? You're the hardest worker I have and a close friend. There's no reason to be concerned."

"Then I don't understand. Why do you want to talk to me?"

The woman sighed heavily. "The Grand Opening was a big success, offering potentials larger than I ever dreamed. I have a group coming in later this morning to do a walk-through."

A shudder ran down her arms. "Are you selling your vineyard?"

"No, no, nothing like that." Margaret shook her head. "They're a distributor. Possibly offering a large—make that a very, very large—as in out of this world contract."

"Are you going to take it?"

Margaret studied her. "That's going to depend."

"On what?"

"On you. To fulfill their orders, we'll need to boost production. I need a strong leader... someone I can trust." The lady grew silent, as if she was waiting for the words to sink in.

"You want me to help train someone else, is that it?"

"No. The leader that I need is... you, Becky. Would you be willing to help me?"

Rebecca's chest was suddenly cold. "What could I do? I'm... I don't understand how I could help. I've never been a boss. I'm just a worker."

Margaret reached across the desk and touched her hand. "Becky, you're smart and intelligent. Fair, level-headed and you understand how things work. You know how to process the fruits and get the winemaking started."

"But Maggie... I think you over-estimate me. I can't do this."

The other woman looked away. "Then I'll have to tell them no."

Rebecca was surprised when Margaret spun her chair away. Rebecca could have sworn she heard the other lady sob.

"Are you okay?"

Silence, but Rebecca knew something wasn't right. She walked around the desk and touched her friend's arm. "Maggie?"

Margaret wiped her cheeks. "I'm sorry. That wasn't right of me to try and force you into a position you don't want."

"What about Isaac? He's the most intelligent man I've ever met. And he told me he was a Marine. He'd make a great leader."

"Isaac will have other duties. If I decide to go forward, we'll need lots of new equipment. I was planning on putting him in charge of the new addition. I figured with the two of you working together to run the operation, we'd have a real chance of success."

*Isaac and I working together? Wait, did I hear her right?* "You're adding on?"

Margaret studied her. The other woman looked exhausted. "I don't know. It's a tough decision." Her boss's expression now seemed to show uncertainty. "Becky, am I going too fast?"

"I, I don't know. Isn't this your dream?"

"Yes, well, part of it. I just feel so confused."

*Confused? Maggie?* This woman was the sharpest lady she'd ever met. It was clear what Rebecca needed to do. "And it would help you if I did as you asked? Would that make you happy?" She swallowed hard. "If that helps you, Maggie, then you can count on me. I'll do it."

Her boss raised an eyebrow. "Why would you change your mind?"

"Because you're my friend and you need me. When our Lord laid down His life, He did it for the sake of others, not to glorify Himself. Jesus gave us an example we all should follow."

"I'm sorry, but I don't understand."

"In humility, God wants us to put others first. Because of Jesus's example, I'm putting your needs ahead of my fears. Now tell me how to help you."

Margaret's chin trembled and then she moved forward and hugged Rebecca. "Thank you. Good and devoted friends like you are difficult to come by. It's a great opportunity for you, by the way."

"Then I should thank you."

Margaret turned away and muttered quietly, but loud enough that Rebecca heard her words. "I wish *he* would have been as faithful as you."

*Was she talking about Mr. Rohrer?* How many times had Margaret said he was her rock? A light began flashing in Rebecca's mind. "Did something happen between you and your friend?"

Margaret looked at the floor. "He went out with another woman."

"What? Are you sure?"

Her boss didn't look up, but slowly nodded.

"I'm sure this is only a misunderstanding. Maggie, I don't have much experience in this, but even I can see Mr. Rohrer is in love with you."

Margaret's eyes were watery. "I thought so as well. But if that is true, tell me this. Why did he spend the night with her?"

*\*\*\**

Margaret had never been more nervous in her life as she watched the van stop in front of her shop. This deal, if everything went well, could make her business an overnight financial success. But there were major risks and hurdles to overcome. The rapid addition of not only equipment, but staff, was intimidating. Luckily, she had Isaac and Rebecca to help her. She turned, finding the pair smiling at her.

"Whatcha want us to do, boss?" Isaac's grin was goofy.

"First, take off that ridiculous hat."

"What do you have against the Vikings?"

"The Vikings were a bunch of ruthless, murdering plunderers. To emulate such people is ludicrous."

"They're a football team, not a bunch of invaders."

"Isaac..."

Margaret caught the glimpse of the wink he shot at his Amish co-worker. "You going to make Becky take off her cap as well?"

"Isaac, her head covering is part of her beliefs. There is no comparison between her show of religious freedom and you wearing that, that... expression of pathetic worship of overgrown men playing a game."

"I see, no to the Vikes, huh? I have a Twins cap in the truck... Leslie gave it to me last week." Margaret couldn't help but grin. The other two laughed.

Rebecca was looking at Margaret, but spoke to Isaac. "You know, Golden, you made her smile."

"That's what friends are for. Right, boss?"

Shaking her head, Margaret responded, "With friends like you two, who needs enemies?"

The bell on the front door rang. Margaret swallowed hard. "Show time."

For the next half hour, the trio led the potential customers through the operation. Margaret encouraged both Rebecca and Isaac to talk about their roles. Standing just inside the upper bay, Rebecca was doing a great job explaining the care that went into preparing the fruit for strawberry wine.

The whole presentation was going very well until Isaac's phone rang. He silenced it, but it immediately resonated a second time with a different tone.

"Please turn that thing off," she whispered.

"Okay, I'll..." He was immediately silent and his face turned pale. "Be right back. This is urgent." He stepped outside.

*What was he doing?* And at a time like this? Rebecca was finishing up when Isaac returned.

The man cleared his throat. "Excuse me for the interruption, everyone." Isaac turned to face Margaret. "I need you to come outside with me for a moment, Ms. Campbell."

Her face felt like it was on fire. "Mr. Golden, can't you see—"

*Doesn't he know how important this is to me?* That was when she noticed it. Something really had shaken Isaac. "If everyone would excuse us for a moment. Maggie, please. It's urgent." Isaac motioned with his head to Rebecca. "I think you better come as well."

Within seconds, the three of them were standing in the bright sunshine. "This better be important."

"I'm sorry, boss, but Henry reached out to me with a request."

Dread peeled off of him like a wet shirt. "What did my brother have to say?" Isaac and Rebecca exchanged a glance.

"He wants me to take you to him."

"At a time like this? Why?"

"There's been a horrible car accident."

*Please, not today.* "Was anyone hurt?"

"Henry's wife Ellie was trapped in the vehicle. They got her out and rushed her to the hospital. Your brother said they're not sure she's going to make it."

# Chapter Seventeen

*Tuesday, Just Before Noon*

Margaret was out of breath from running all the way from outside as she entered the Emergency Department. She scanned the waiting room until she found him. Henry was sitting alone in a corner, head down. She ran to him. "Henry?"

He quickly stood and held her in his arms. "Margaret. Thank you for coming. It's been, it's been bloody terrible, this miserable wait. I wish they'd tell me what's going on with my wife."

"What happened?"

"The police said a pickup truck ran the light at the intersection of Route 896 and the Lincoln Highway at high speed. T-boned the Expedition and forced it into the path of a tractor trailer. The truck hit her head on." He wiped the moisture from his face. "It took them almost an hour to extract her from the wreckage."

*Oh God, please don't take her. She's like a sister to me.* "How is Ellie?"

"As far as I know, she's still alive, but they're not sure of the outcome. Touch and go was what they told me."

"Any word on the baby?"

There were tears in Henry's eyes. "The nurse wouldn't answer me. Margaret, I don't know what to do." He clung tightly to her. "Ellie's my entire world. How can I go on if she dies?"

The figure of her brother was blurry before her. "Quit talking like that. You need to have faith."

"Faith? My wife's somewhere in this hospital and I don't even know... Suppose she dies? And our son? They wouldn't even tell me if he'll survive."

"What? A, a son? You're having a son? How long have you known?"

Henry sat down and rubbed his nose. "Our curiosity got the better of us two weeks ago. He was so active. I would put my head against her stomach and talk to my boy. And he'd kick back! I looked forward to holding him. Raising him, teaching him to be a man. And now..." His voice trailed off and his body quaked.

"Don't give up hope." Memories came flooding back to her. It seemed like only yesterday when Ellie had been missing—she'd disappeared in Hawaii. How hopeless everything had seemed... She held his hand. "We've been in worse situations before. Do you remember?"

"No. What could be more miserable than this?"

Margaret brushed Henry's hair from his eyes. "When Ellie was missing and everyone said she was dead. But against all hope, we believed... and found her." Her brother's chin was trembling. "And together, we rescued her, didn't we? You and I, we were a great team."

"But she's not imprisoned on some island. She's fighting for her life on some cold, sterile bed, with no one by her side. The situation's hopeless. What could either of us possibly do?"

"We can be here for her when she wakes up." Margaret squeezed his hand. "Ellie will make it, Henry." Her brother focused on a spot on the floor. "Where's the rest of the family?"

"Don't you remember? Oh, that's right. You don't come to the family get togethers anymore. Edmund, Tara and their daughters left for Orlando on Sunday. Harry and Ashley flew to California yesterday. The two of them have a meeting with someone about a book deal. Of course, Mum's at home with our girls, and Sophie is home resting. Did you know she gave birth to a daughter on Sunday?"

Margaret bristled at the sound of that witch's name. *Bet the new child looks like you, too.* "No, I didn't." She hesitated briefly before continuing. "I asked about the family. Why'd you include her?"

He studied her face. "You know the answer. After Ellie, she's the second-best friend I've ever had. When Ellie was missing, she gave me strength. Never let me down."

*What am I? Leftovers from a week ago?* Margaret could feel her blood pressure increase. "Perhaps you forgot, but I was there with you, too, searching for Ellie... in person. Stayed right by your side until we brought her home."

Henry's face and voice showed agitation. "My wife's fighting for her life somewhere in this hospital and you want to argue about where you are in the pecking order of my life? What happened to the kind and loving sister who was the darling of the family? Did all that education and your new California friends give you this air of superiority and place a chip on your shoulder?"

Margaret's face heated. "I look down on no one. Perhaps it is *you* who has changed."

"If that's what you truly believe, I'm going to buy you a mirror so you can see for yourself." Henry shook his head. "Know what? I don't have time for this. My wife deserves my full attention right now."

*If only you would honor Ellie all the time.* The duplicity of the situation rubbed her raw. If he truly loved Ellie, why did Sophie's children look exactly like Henry? It was time to ask...

She became aware of a woman standing before them, dressed in scrubs. "Are you Mr. Campbell?"

Despite the moisture that suddenly appeared on his cheeks, Henry stood tall. "Yes, I am. Are you the doctor who's caring for my wife, Ellie Campbell?"

The lady appeared to be exhausted. "I'm just one of many. Her injuries were traumatic."

"Please tell me, how is she?"

"Definitely a fighter. Your wife is in the ICU now. She's still in serious condition, but at least she's stable."

Margaret reached for Henry's hand. He squeezed hers so tightly, she thought her fingers would fall off. "Thank God. And the child?" Henry's entire body was quivering.

The woman took a deep breath before continuing. "The baby was in distress. We had no choice but to

176

take him by Caesarian. Your son is in the NICU, which is our neonatal intensive care unit. I can take you back if you want to meet him."

Her brother shook his head with a vengeance. "I want to see my wife first." Henry's pitch was high and he palmed his eyes again. "Thank you for saving Ellie's life. She's everything to me. I don't... don't know.... How could I ever... "

Patting his hand, the doctor comforted him. "It's okay. Let me take you to her." The woman turned to Margaret. "I'm sorry, but we only allow one visitor at a time."

"I understand." She again hugged her brother. She wanted to say something, anything, but the words wouldn't come.

Henry pulled her against him, very tightly. "Thank you for being here."

"Give Ellie my love."

"Done." Henry released her and the pair disappeared behind the hallway doors.

Margaret's thoughts and prayers were for Ellie and her nephew. That is, until the rapid clicking of heels on terrazzo interrupted. Turning, Margaret faced the intruder who violated her solitude. A woman Margaret did, but then again didn't, really know—Sophia Miller.

\*\*\*

Before Margaret could do anything, Sophie threw her arms around Margaret. And like most times, Sophie's tears were plentiful. *Such a drama queen.* Standing there, Margaret kept her arms at her side.

It was a few seconds before the other woman quit blubbering and spoke. "How's Ellie?"

"The doctor said she was stable."

"And my poor Henry? How is he?"

*My* poor Henry? *That was the last straw.* Through gritted teeth, Margaret spit out the hissed words. "This is a place for family, not homewreckers."

Sophia recoiled. "A homewrecker? What are you talking about?"

"As if you didn't know. Why are you here?"

"I'm here for my best friends. They need me."

*Self-centered prima donna.* "Henry and Ellie need you like a sinking ship needs a screen door on the keel."

The comment seemed to cut deep, to poke a hole in the other's self-inflated view of her importance. "Wh-why would you even say something like that?"

"You think I'm stupid, don't you?"

"Margaret, what's wrong?"

Margaret's anger was boiling over, to the point where she felt like punching Sophie. "You, that's what. Since I've moved home, I've watched you weave your evil webs. I know you've drawn Henry deep into your lair. I can see that, despite all that you have, you want the one thing that should be out of your reach... my brother."

Somehow, the deflated expression on Sophie's face wasn't nearly as satisfying as Margaret had hoped. The silent cascade of liquid from her eyes was starting to puddle on the floor. "Why are you so angry at me? What did I do?"

Margaret's lips were wet, so she rubbed her mouth with her hand. Ignoring the question,

Margaret continued. "You have no honor, no conscience. Kissing my brother like you do, and not caring who sees. You call Ellie your 'best friend', and then hang all over her husband like a female dog in heat. And if I hear you tell my brother you love him one more time, I'll slap you silly."

"Please don't do this." Sophie was trembling—no, shaking—almost uncontrollably. "You don't understand."

"I understand perfectly! You seduced my brother, on multiple occasions apparently."

Margaret watched as the color drained from her adversary's face. She also took note that everyone in the waiting room was watching with keen interest. The shaky voice caught her attention. "Is that what you think? That I'm some, some... tart?"

"You're worse than that. You're a two-faced, backstabbing whore who's sleeping with her best friend's husband."

Sophie grabbed her arms, but Margaret ripped free. "You're wrong. Henry and I, we've never slept together. That's not the kind of love we have."

"Really?" Margaret hesitated so the sarcasm could drip to the floor. "Then tell me why your boys all look exactly like Henry did when he was a wee one. They have his red hair and green eyes." Margaret took a step closer. "And I'd bet my vineyard there's not a single redhead in the Miller family tree. You may have everyone else fooled, but I know the facts. I'm not nearly as naïve and simple as you think. I know those boys were fathered by my brother."

The woman's whole body was trembling now. "Do you know the truth?"

"Truth? Truth? Coming from you? I'll never believe a single word you ever say again. I hate you, you shameless little—"

The deep voice was full of anger. "That's enough, Margaret."

She whipped around to find her brother standing there. He quickly moved until he stood between Margaret and *that* woman.

Henry was seething. "What gives you the right to judge others without knowing the whole situation? Does it make you feel good to run someone else down?"

"I know she seduced you. And that her boys are your sons."

"Sophie and Benjamin are their parents."

*Why is he denying it?* Those boys were the spitting image of her brother. "And she's got you lying to cover for her. You do realize the woman you married is here, in a hospital bed, but you're more concerned at this moment about your lover."

"I am painfully aware of where my wife is."

"Then why are you here instead of at her side? Oh, I see. You had to come down here in case Sophie came, didn't you? Maybe I've got it wrong. Perhaps Sophie didn't seduce you. I think you're both equally to blame. Am I correct?"

"Who made you judge, jury and executioner? With all that education, I can't believe how idiotic you're acting right now. Let me give you some brotherly advice 101. *Mind your own business.*"

"My family is my business."

"You don't deserve this family or the blessings laid upon your table. I want you to leave. Now."

Margaret took a few deep breaths. "Not until I see Ellie."

"Why? So you can jump all over her like you did Sophie? Going on with your conspiracy theories? I think not."

"No. I just want to make sure she's all right."

"Ellie's in a lot of pain. They gave her medication for her comfort. She needs her rest."

"Then I'll wait to see her. Or do you plan on bullying me to leave?"

Her peripheral vision caught the movement. Two uniformed security guards approached them. The younger man was obviously in charge. "What's going on here?"

Henry assessed him before answering. "We were having a discussion."

The guard moved closer. "From what I was told, it was an argument. You have two choices. All of you can either calm down... or I can remove you." The arrogance of the man was evident. He eyed Henry up and down. "Forcibly if I have to."

Margaret saw the anger flare in her brother's eyes. The guard obviously didn't have a clue who he was talking to. Her brother may have been retired, but no amount of time could take the Royal Marine out of him. Yet instead of meeting the guard's challenge, Henry nodded and smiled sweetly. "We didn't mean to cause a scene, officer. There will be no more problems or disturbances from us. You have my word on it."

The guard swiveled and faced Margaret. "How about you? Are you going to behave?"

Before she answered, her gaze fell on her brother. No matter what his words had been, she knew his resolve. And from behind him came a noise. The sound of Sophie crying. A pang of guilt rose within her. *What have I done?*

"I'm waiting for an answer, young lady."

"Sorry, sir. I'll be quieter."

"Well then. My work here is done. Don't make me have to come back over here. Now, have a good day."

The pair shuffled off. Brother and sister stared at each other. Henry spoke first. "They want to allow Ellie some time to rest. It will be hours before she wakes. I think it would be in both of our best interests if you left."

"But Henry, I want to—"

"You've done enough damage. Please don't make it worse. I'm asking you to leave, please? There's a time and a place to finish our conversation. It isn't now."

Margaret stepped to the side so she could stare at Sophie. "What about her? Is she leaving as well?"

"No. Sophie's not going anywhere."

"Oh, I see. Your own sister has to go while your lover stays... all while you wait for your wife to wake up. So much for the blood is thicker than water theory."

She could not only see, but she could sense Henry's sadness. "I pity you, Margaret. Maybe someday you'll find out what it means to have true friendship... people who stick with you through triumph and disaster. People who always take your feelings into consideration before theirs. One day, when you find that, you'll finally understand. Goodbye."

Henry turned and placed an arm around Sophie's shoulder. He led her to a different corner of the room before they sat down. *Understand what? Friendship?* Like she and Joe had... or used to have? The emptiness in her heart suddenly ached.

Margaret extracted her phone from her pocket. Joe's smile shone brightly on the screen. No messages, no texts from him. She quickly composed and sent a text to him.

Having a horrid day. I really need you.
Where in God's name are you?

# Chapter Eighteen

*A Week Later*

The scent of baked apple pie radiating from the candle warmers filled the showroom. Becky's idea of a homey aroma to welcome the customers. A couple dozen emails were waiting on the laptop. Orders, inquiries and delivery confirmations filled the inbox.

Margaret quickly scanned, hoping to find something from Joe. This was the second week since he'd disappeared and the emptiness in her heart was larger than she could imagine. *Why didn't I tell him while I had the chance?* And now it was too late. After the letter his friend Daisy had given her, it was plain that their relationship was over. No matter what she wanted.

A sharp noise from the upper floor interrupted her thoughts, but only for a moment. Then the argument about what to do next rolled on between her heart and her mind. *Reach out to him and patch this up.* That would be her heart and then her mind chimed in. *But he cheated on me, blatantly.* Her heart was winning the debate. Margaret grabbed her cell phone and touched the home button. The image was there—of the two of them in front of the daylilies. Joe's gentle smile haunted her. *How could you leave me?*

The jingle of the showroom door interrupted her pity party. The new girl Margaret hired to staff the shop was in the back room. Rebecca had needed assistance loading cases for a shipment. *Needed a break anyway.* Pushing back her chair, she left her office to greet the guest. It was a woman with blonde hair. She was perusing the fruit wines.

"May I help you?" When the woman turned, Margaret's mouth went dry as she recognized the lady. It was *her*.

"Hi. Wait, we met at the grand opening. You're the vine master, aren't you?" The lady extended her hand. "I'm Georgia. Do you remember me?"

*All too well.* This was the woman who had seduced and spent the night with Joe. It was difficult to be civil, but Margaret made a valiant effort. "I think so. You bought a bottle that day. Did you enjoy it?" *Too bad you didn't choke on it.*

"It was delightful. Wonderful bouquet. Seasoned aroma. Excellent taste. But I want to get a different flavor today. I had blackberry last time."

"Up for a change?" *How about moving to Mars?*

"Yep. Although I thoroughly enjoyed it, that flavor wasn't very lucky for me."

*Yeah, because Joe's gone.* "What do you mean?"

"I bought it because I wanted the night to be special. But the evening didn't turn out anything like I'd hoped."

*Huh?* "I don't understand."

"Oh, I was supposed to go out on a date with a man. One I really, really liked." She gave Margaret a quizzical look. "You probably know him. He was tending your tasting bar. Dr. Joseph Rohrer. Know who I mean?"

*Better than you'd ever imagine.* "Yes, yes I do. Did something go wrong?"

Georgia frowned. "He cancelled our date."

Margaret felt as if she'd just been drenched with a bucket of ice water. *He broke off the date? What?* "Why would he do that?"

"Joe apologized and told me he wasn't free. That he shouldn't have asked me out because he was in a long-term relationship. Then he confessed how much he was in love with someone else. But what he said next confused me."

Her knees were shaking. "What did Joe tell you?"

"He said he couldn't betray her. He loved her too much to even consider it. Wasn't that an odd thing to say?"

Margaret's whole body trembled. She whispered, "Oh my God. He didn't spend the night with you, did he?"

"What? Why would you... oh no." Georgia's face paled. "It's you, isn't it? You're the girl he was talking about, aren't you?"

*Oh God. I was wrong about him.* Everything grew blurry. Her heart spoke loudly. *See? I told you so.* "Y-yes, I am. I'm the girl Joe loves."

***

Leslie stepped into the shop holding the carryout tray of mochas in her hands. A woman walked toward her. "Good afternoon. Welcome to the Scottish Lass Vineyards. May I help you?"

"No, thanks. I'm just here to see Maggie."

"Okay. Have a good day."

Leslie paused before knocking on the office door. Isaac had mentioned how Margaret seemed to have changed since the grand opening. How her ever-present smile was gone, replaced with a frown filled with sadness. He stated it seemed their dear friend was aging right before his eyes. *Lord, help me lift my friend's spirit. Place the right words in my mouth.* After a deep breath, Leslie knocked on the door.

"It's open."

Entering the room, she was greeted by the back of the big desk chair. Margaret was facing the window. "Hey, kiddo. I was in the neighborhood and when I looked on the passenger seat, there were four café mochas. I figured, being the kind, loving, devoted wife and friend that I am, I'd share. Hope you don't mind, but I stopped upstairs and gave one to both Isaac and Becky. That left two more, so I was hoping you and I could take a moment and polish off the last two. Whatcha think?"

The other woman didn't turn around. "That was nice, but I'm not sure I'd be the best company right now. Maybe you should go upstairs and take a few minutes to be with your husband." Margaret's voice dropped to a whisper and Leslie was sure the words she heard weren't intended for her ears. "At least you have one."

After setting the tray on the desk, Leslie walked around until she faced her friend. "Maggie? Are you okay? What's wrong?"

Margaret wiped her cheeks. "My dream came true."

"Is that a bad thing?"

"This one was. You see, the day we opened, I had this dream that business took off and exceeded my wildest dreams."

Leslie watched Margaret's eyes. There was misery in them. "From what Isaac said, business is booming."

Nodding her head, Margaret continued. "We've almost got more business than we can handle. I'm sure your husband mentioned we're expanding."

"Yes, he did. Is that what's wrong?" Leslie offered the leading question, hoping Margaret would open up. But Leslie knew better. *Joe's the problem.*

"No. There was a second part to the dream... Nightmare, really. I became so hooked on success that I lost everything. My family, the closeness with you and Isaac, my friendship with Becky."

Leslie knelt and pulled Margaret into a hug. "Nonsense, Maggie. We're friends for life. Isaac and I aren't going anywhere." She squeezed the other woman tightly when she heard her sob. "It was only a nightmare. Wait and see. It won't come true."

Margaret pulled away. "Part of it already has." Reaching for a tissue, she continued. "The worst part of the dream was that I, I, lost Joe." Another sob. "And it came true."

Voices from the showroom drifted in. Leslie closed the door and took a seat across the desk from her friend. Margaret rotated her chair to face her. "It was his fault. I don't know what happened between the two of you that day, but he never should have asked that woman out. And he did it in front of you. I know him well enough to see he was only making a point. Still, that was hateful and wrong."

Margaret's eyes slowly raised until they met Leslie's. "He didn't come home that night. I assumed he spent the night with her."

"Oh, Maggie..."

"He came to me later and wanted to talk about what happened. I told him words wouldn't make a difference. I was so sure he betrayed me." Margaret wiped the corners of her mouth with the tissue. "That woman, Georgia, stopped by today. Know what she told me?"

*I'm afraid to ask.* "No, what?"

"Joe stood her up. Told her he was involved with someone else. Someone he loved. And I knew right then, it was me. But I'd been too blind to see it."

Margaret's eyes dropped to the desk. She touched her phone and Leslie saw the image. Of the two of them in his backyard garden. Leslie kept her words quiet. "Isaac and I knew he was in love with you. And the joy that was in your face, we were sure you loved him, too."

"Looking back and analyzing my heart, I was. I still am. Yet, I neglected the one thing I needed most in life because I chased some stupid thing I wanted. Success won... love lost. Now Joe's gone and it's over."

"You still love him, don't you?"

Margaret nodded. "I always will."

"You know, Maggie, I admire you. You're so intelligent and talented. You can do whatever you want. I mean, a year ago, this was an old farm field and now look at it. Your dream came to life. Now you need to focus on another dream, the dream of love. It's time to get back together with Joe. You can patch things up. It's not too late."

Margaret studied her with watery eyes. "Afraid it is." She pulled a paper from her pocket and tossed it across the desk. "He had his friend Daisy stop by to give me this. Read it."

Her friend spun the chair away so she again faced the window.

Leslie unfolded the paper, quickly recognizing Joe Rohrer's longhand.

Dear Margaret,

I'm sorry for everything that happened. I know you feel I betrayed you and for that I beg your forgiveness. I regret many things in my life. God knows I'm the biggest fool He ever created, but the thing that pains me the most is that I've hurt you. You are special – the most vibrant, wonderful and loving person I've ever met. I regret that I never got to tell you in person that I love you, but I do. And because of how I feel, I can't risk running into you again. I know I've squandered the greatest gift God ever sent my way. I hurt you and that was unconscionable.

Analyzing everything, I realize I've made a mess of things, yet again. I prayed and prayed, asking God to help. He answered my prayers, quickly. I need a fresh start. I'm sure you've heard about the humanitarian mission to the Philippines. I volunteered. And when that's over, I'm not coming back to Lancaster. I'm not sure what's next, but I'm willing to follow whatever path God leads me on. I just know it won't be Lancaster.

I've asked Daisy to liquidate my assets. I know you've been looking for a house. You once told me that the home you and I shared was perfect in your eyes. Stay there as long as you want. I'd really like you to buy it, but it's your choice. I've told Daisy to make you an offer you can't refuse.

Saying goodbye to you is the hardest thing I'll ever do. Somehow, I'll survive without getting that first kiss I wanted. Or hearing your response when I proposed someday. Growing old with you is just a pipedream I'll cherish until I die. But not having my best friend and soulmate by my side... my heart is permanently shattered. God offered me the heaven of your love and like the fool I am, I threw it away.

I wish you success and happiness. But above all, I hope you find the love of your life and love that man for all eternity. You deserve the best, and we both know it wasn't me.

You told me words couldn't fix this, so this is our final goodbye. Someday, when you've made all your dreams come true, remember me and how I loved you. For I will always love you, Margaret Campbell. Until the day God calls me home.

Love, forever and eternal, Joe

"And like that he leaves?"

The chair spun around again until they were face to face. "What can I do? It's over. Even I can read the unspoken words in there. 'We're through.' I've lost him for good."

"No, no, no. Maggie, you can do anything if you have enough faith."

"That tank is pretty empty today."

"Then let's fill it up. I'll help you."

Once again, Margaret turned her chair away. "Thanks anyway, Leslie, but it's too late. I've already given up."

## Chapter Nineteen

*The Following Saturday*

The leaves were starting to change on some of the trees along the golf course. The vivid tones of the mums she and Joe had planted provided a bright contrast to the dark, late summer green of the oaks in the backyard. The evening sky was picturesque as the last rays of sunshine turned the clouds to hues of orange, silver and black.

Margaret searched for the first star, so she could make a wish upon it. Her mind drifted back to the early years of her life, when she lived in Scotland. Pops would hold her in his arms as the night sky came to life. Tight in his embrace, together they would make a wish. But now, her father was gone. And so was Joe.

Thoughts of him consumed Margaret's mind constantly. And she prayed for his safety. The super storm that had ravaged the Philippines had thrown the islands into chaos. Most basic services, such as electricity and drinkable water were unavailable. And amid that chaos, civility had broken down.

Looting, gangs and violence were what the news showed. Margaret had to quit watching after the service reported the cold-blooded murder of a team of UN aid workers from Europe. Executed just to steal the supplies they carried.

Even though he was eight thousand miles away, Margaret could still feel Joe's presence. It was impossible not to. A friendship as deep as they'd experienced didn't just end neatly. Tendrils of feelings, and love, were still there. Some wounds would never heal.

Margaret had no idea if Joe had his phone with him or whether, if he did, if cell service was available. But she texted him daily. *I need you badly, my friend.* Her world was crumbling around her. She hadn't contacted anyone in her family since the blowout at the hospital. And they hadn't reached out to her. The only stability in her life was the vineyard. *If I would have put the effort into our relationship instead of the business...* No sense going there because Margaret couldn't change the past. Instead, she prayed Joe would return to her.

The honking sound of a pair of Canadian geese drew her attention. They appeared almost nightly. Margaret smiled sadly when she remembered the story. Joe had told her they nested along the Cocalico Creek. "Local yokels" was what he called them. When the pair flew over in the evenings, he'd joked they were going out to dinner. Together, they'd even named them Mabel and George. Unwillingly, she found herself reaching for his hand, but of course he wasn't there. *Joe, why can't you...*

The shrill ring of her cell interrupted her thoughts. She read the screen. *Hannah's Bakery? Why would they call me on a Saturday night?* Hannah's Bakery was one of her vendors. Thinking it was probably a mistake, Margaret declined the call. The owner, Hannah Espenshade, was a kind and friendly lady. The essence of happiness. All because of the love she and her husband shared. *I'd be happy as well if Joe was here with me. But instead, he had to run off to help others.*

It rang again. *Maybe it's an emergency.* Margaret answered. "Hello?"

There was so much noise in the background that it was hard to make out the words. "Maggie? It's Hannah. Can you come over to Didi's house? We're having an impromptu party. Can you make it?"

The last thing Margaret wanted tonight was to attend a happy event. "I'm not sure. I mean it's a Saturday night and, this is so sudden."

"Oh, I can guarantee you don't want to miss this. Something wonderful happened to Didi and we're all celebrating with her. Please come. For Didi's sake? I know you two have a close friendship. Please?"

*Close friendship? I wish my best friend would remember we had one of those.* "Okay. I'll get changed and be there soon."

After she hung up, Margaret pondered the conversation with Hannah. *"Something wonderful happened to Didi?"* What did that mean? It suddenly dawned on her. Didi was a highly acclaimed newscaster. She had shared with Margaret how one of the other networks had reached out to her, inquiring if she was interested in joining their news team. *My nightmare continues.* Didi would be moving on, probably to New York or Washington or LA. *I'm losing another dear friend.*

Before she knew it, Margaret was parked in front of Didi's home. The street was crowded with cars. An old Ford pickup arrived and parked right behind her. The classic belonged to Isaac Golden. He yelled a greeting before running around to the other side of the truck to open the door for his wife, Leslie. The woman sprinted over and embraced Margaret. "Did you hear the good news?"

*What, does everyone know what's happening but me?* "No. What is it?"

Leslie started to speak, but Isaac interrupted her. "Now Buttercup, it's not your story to tell. It would be better if Didi told Maggie herself."

Margaret's eyes shifted between the pair. "I think I figured it out, and while I'm happy for Didi, I'm sad for myself. Maybe that's being greedy, but I'll miss her friendship."

The married couple shared a strange look before Leslie stepped closer to Margaret. "What do you think it is?"

"Didi told me she was offered a network job. I think she took it. That's the happy news."

Again, the Goldens turned to each other. But this time, laughter erupted between the pair.

*Why are they laughing, at my expense?* "Okay, if my guess wasn't right, what's going on?"

Leslie opened her mouth to speak until Isaac lowered his voice. "Buttercup..."

Leslie turned to shoot a death stare at her husband before focusing on her friend. "Fine. Come with me." Leslie grabbed Margaret's hand and pulled as they ran to the front door. "Come on. Let's hurry. I can't wait to see the look on your face when she tells you."

Leslie knocked and within seconds, the door flew open. Margaret recognized the man as Phil Phillips, Didi's father. "Come on in and enjoy the celebration. We can't wait—"

Holding up her finger, Leslie interrupted him. "Maggie doesn't know, yet. Can you have your daughter share the good news? I want to see Maggie's face when she finds out."

The man's smile widened. "Absolutely. Just a sec..." He turned and held his hand to his mouth so he could direct the soundwaves. "Diedre! There's someone here who wants to know what this is all about."

Didi came running down the hall, sliding the last ten feet of the hardwood floor in her socks. Margaret had never seen such a huge smile on Didi's face. "Maggie!" Her friend engulfed Margaret in a hug and squeezed so tightly that she thought her back would break. "It's a miracle. God answered all my prayers."

Didi released her. Margaret didn't miss the moisture in her friend's eyes. Before Margaret could ask, the young blonde continued. "They found him."

*Him?* It suddenly dawned on her who *him* was. *Didi's husband Luke.* "Are you sure?"

"Yes, yes. It was a positive ID."

*ID? Poor Didi, she's lost it.* Margaret shivered despite the warmth in the house. *They found her husband's remains. Maybe she's happy because this will bring her closure.*

"When will they ship his body back here?"

Didi laughed. "Next week, but I think you must have misunderstood. It's not just his body, it's all of him. Maggie, Luke's *alive!* The military rescued him three days ago. He's recuperating at Landstuhl Medical Center in Germany. My husband is finally coming home. At last I'll get a chance to introduce Luke to his son."

As Didi's news sunk in, the world turned blurry. "I'm so happy for you," was all she could get out.

When Margaret embraced Didi again, the jubilant woman whispered in her ear. "Thank you for all your support, your friendship and for just being there. Maggie, friends like you are what got me through the pain of the last three years. Friends who have become family. I can't wait to introduce you to Luke."

Another knock sounded on the door and Didi moved on to share her news with the next guest. Immense sadness filled Margaret's heart. She jumped when Leslie touched her shoulder. Her friend looked concerned. "Are you okay?"

"Yes. Of course."

Leslie studied her eyes. "Fibber. I can read you like a book. You're thinking that now you took Didi's place."

*What?* "I don't understand what you mean."

"Now you're the one waiting for your man to come home."

Margaret quickly turned away so Leslie wouldn't see. "Waiting for Joe to return? That's nonsense. I've never been happier. I'm going to see if I can find Hannah." As she walked away from Leslie, Joe's face flashed before her eyes. *Three years without you would drive me crazy. You better come back to me, soon. I need you, Joe, desperately.*

\*\*\*

The increasing roar of the jet engine shook the silence of the early morning. Joe watched as the F-18 Super Hornet catapulted off the deck into flight. It was 1:15 A.M. and sleep was not on the menu. Just like every night, his insomnia, or maybe his conscience, refused to let him sleep. Joe rubbed his chin, noting the stubble. *Need to shave before today's mission.* The next fighter lifted into the sky. The aircraft carrier was changing out her combat air patrol. As soon as this flight of warbirds got aloft, the ship would collect the planes that were currently on duty.

Looking out to sea, he could detect another ship, moving slowly through the night in a never-ending vigilance to protect the super-carrier he stood on. That ship in the night was one of the destroyers in the George Washington's carrier battle group. Joe shook his head. When he arrived with the other volunteers from the States, he assumed they would all work together. But the UN, which supposedly controlled the response, using mainly American assets, had assigned all of the American volunteers to the hospital ship USNS Comfort. All but one. To his surprise, Joe Rohrer had been sent to assist the medical team on CVN-73, the George Washington.

"Morning, sir."

Joe turned and nodded to the young sailor who also stood on the deck next to him. "Morning, Oliver." The kid was fresh out of basic training. He worked in the galley, helping prepare food for the six thousand hungry mouths on this floating city. The boy kept him company almost every morning, before heading below deck to stand his watch.

They observed as the carrier launched another plane. "Wish that was you down there, doc?"

"Some days I do." Becoming a fighter pilot had been Joe's dream since he was a boy. And it had been right within his reach. But Joe had backed out of the Naval Academy at the last minute so he could study pre-med at Pitt. And the rest was history.

"I think you made the right decision, becoming a doctor. I mean, you get to help people every day. Making a real difference for all humanity."

Joe laughed. It wasn't the first time the boy had exposed his philosophical side. "I don't know. Maybe I should have gone to the academy. You know, 'it's not a job, it's an adventure'. I could have been off saving the world."

"You are, doc, just in a different way. For me, Navy service is a means to an end. This is how I'm paying for college, so I can study philosophy."

They fell silent. Joe's mind drifted to the east, to the girl he loved, but would never get to hold. *Maggie, I love you.* But he wasn't the right man for her. His track record supported his thoughts. *Save the world? All I do is hurt the ones I love.* And because of how much he loved Margaret, he needed to stay away from Lancaster. He wasn't strong enough to keep his resolve. If he saw Margaret again, he'd cave. In a second.

The device in his pocket vibrated again, like it did about this time every morning. He retrieved it and quickly read her message. It would have been less heartbreaking if Margaret forgot about him. But she didn't. Margaret texted him at least three times a day. Most texts gave him little glimpses into what was happening in Lancaster. But this one had a different feel.

Joe,

Believe it or not, I pray for your safety every day. I received surprising news yesterday—Didi's husband is alive and will be back in Lancaster next week. (I felt miserably guilty because I wish it were you who was coming home – to me.)

I shared with you about the big blow-up with Henry and Sophie in the hospital waiting room. And because of that, I can't go see Ellie. She's the closest I'll ever come to having a sister. And I'm neglecting her. (I can't seem to do anything right, can I?) It's no wonder no one in my family has reached out to me. They hate me and have every right to do so.

I know I should go see Ellie, but I'm afraid of facing my family alone. I'm so scared and weak. Why can't you be here to help me? I need your friendship in the worst way.

Can you please call me? I feel like if I don't hear your voice, I'll die.

Though you never told me in person, I know you love me, or at least did. If you still feel anything,

anything at all in your heart for me, please reach out to me.

It's probably too late to say this, but I love you, Joe. I wish I'd have told you in person. My greatest prayer is that you still love me too.

Please respond to me, in some way, in any way at all. Before I lose the rest of my mind.

In case you missed it, I love you, Joe. I always will.

Your Maggie

*What should I do?* Out of all the women he'd loved before, what he felt for Margaret was so much more. And because of that, he couldn't risk hurting her again. *But how can I turn my back on my best friend?* Maggie needs me. *Yet, If I screw up again, I'll just hurt her.*

The voice seemed to come from the morning wind. *Quit being so self-centered. You claim you love her, but then act like this? Love is more than just words, it's actions. You know what to do and if you don't, you're a damned fool, Joseph Rohrer.*

He whipped around to face Oliver. "What did you say?"

The kid gave him a puzzled look. "Huh? I didn't say anything, sir. Heading down to the galley now. Have a safe day on shore, sir."

"Sorry, Oliver. You, too."

The hum of the warship beneath his feet continued. *What do You want me to do? How can I protect her, but still be her friend? Please show me the way, Lord.* The words had no sooner formed in his mind before a vibrant, bright shooting star cut a path across the northern sky, heading east. East, where eight thousand miles away, Paradise waited.

Another voice spoke inside of him. *Is that clear enough?* He again reached for his cell.

# Chapter Twenty

*Sunday Afternoon*

Margaret's hands were shaking. "I should eat." But there was no hunger, no want of food or drink or anything... but Joe's voice. "Why do I even bother?" He was gone. He didn't acknowledge her texts, wouldn't so much as give her the time of day...

The ringing of her device startled her. When she read the caller ID on the screen, it was as if she was paralyzed. One more ring and it would dump to voicemail. Quickly scooping the device from the table, she managed to connect the call and place the phone next to her ear. "Joe? Is that really you?"

The voice answering the phone was shaky. "Margaret? It is you. It's so good to hear your voice."

"Can you please call me Maggie, like you used to?"

"I will, but I need you to hear this, Maggie. Are you listening?"

Her hands were again shaking, but this time it was out of happiness. "I am."

"I love you, Maggie. Only you. I'm so sorry for my screwup the night of the Grand Opening. I need to tell you nothing happened."

"I know. Georgia came back into the shop. Said she needed a different flavor of wine because the first one was unlucky. Then she told me what you said. That you were in love with someone else. A-a-and that was me, wasn't it?"

"Yes. It was you all along. And I do love you. Can we work this out?"

Margaret rubbed her hand across her cheeks to stop the tears. "I want that more than anything. And Joe, I love you, too."

They spoke for almost two hours, until he had to get ready for his day. And because they'd talked everything out together, she was ready to face her family. Between Didi's words of the strength she drew from her friends and Joe's words of hope, she was prepared to face her kin. She might not agree with what they did, but she would no longer judge them. *Never should have done that.* Instead, she would beg for mercy and forgiveness. Margaret wasn't alone anymore, no longer felt deserted. Joe might be half a world away, but his spirit filled her heart. They'd agreed to talk when he returned to the ship, at seven in the morning, her time.

She parked her Land Rover in front of the sprawling house where Henry and Ellie lived. Despite the determination, there was a shakiness in her limbs when she knocked on the door.

Much to her surprise, her niece and namesake, Maggie May, opened the door. "Auntie Margaret!"

The child hugged her tightly. "We're having a party. Come in."

A coldness rolled down her spine when Margaret followed the child into the living room. The room was filled with children. Little girls who looked like Ellie, and boys that resembled Henry. Sophie, Ben and their children were visiting. All eyes were on her.

"Hi. I was wondering if I could stop by and see Ellie for a moment or two. Would she be up to a visitor?"

Her brother placed the infant he'd been holding in the bassinet before turning to face her. "She just went up to rest, but I'm sure my wife would want to be interrupted... for you." To her astonishment, he threw his arms around her. Even more surprising was how tightly she hugged him back. He whispered in her ear, "I missed you."

"As I did you. Henry..."

He shushed her. "Later. Let me take you to see Ellie."

Leading Margaret up the stairs, memories flooded back to when she had lived here. Together, Margaret and Sophie had designed the bedroom her brother and his wife shared. The recollections stopped when Henry knocked on the door and peeked in. "Honey, you have a visitor."

"Who is it, Henry? I'm pretty tired."

"Maggot's here. Up for a short visit?"

"Yes, yes. Please send her in."

Henry swung the door open, entered and then placed the vanity chair next to Ellie's side of the bed. The woman gave her a twin-dimpled smile and reached out with her left hand. Margaret sat and took it. They sat in silence, looking at each other as they held hands. Margaret's mind drifted back to the day Margaret and Henry had rescued Ellie from the island where she'd been imprisoned. Cuts, welts and bruises had covered most of Ellie's body. She looked as battered today as she had then. Both eyes were black. A piece of tape covered her nose. Casts concealed her right arm and left leg. Scabs from scrapes and abrasions littered most of her exposed skin.

"I'm sorry it took me so long to get here. How are you feeling?"

"Pretty wiped. I don't have a lot of stamina, but thankfully I'm alive. Did you meet our son?"

"Not yet, I was kind of in a hurry to see you and pay my respects. I should have come sooner. It's just..."

"Henry told me what happened."

"I was wrong. Never should have said anything or jumped to conclusions."

Ellie squeezed her hand. "That's okay. It's time you know the secret." Ellie's eyes drifted past Margaret and then the other woman nodded. Margaret turned to find her brother standing there—with Sophie and her husband Ben to his right.

Ellie's voice was soft. "You were correct in seeing the resemblance between your brother and Sophie's boys. It's undeniable."

Ben stepped forward. "Thanks to a genetic defect, I can't father children, but Sophie and I wanted a family. After a lot of soul searching, Sophie and I asked Henry to be the donor. And he agreed. Your brother *is* the biological father of all five of our children."

Ellie continued. "Ben and Sophie are our closest friends. We wanted them to be happy and that was why we decided to go through with it. Henry and I made that decision... together."

Henry came and touched Margaret's arm. "I know what you were thinking, but Sophie and I never slept together. Not even before I met Ellie."

Margaret had trouble looking at them. "I didn't know and I made the mistake of judging you. All of you. I'm sorry." Their explanation had resolved most of the questions in her mind, but... "May I ask one more thing?"

Ben smiled at her. "Does it involve how my wife behaves around your brother? How she tells him she loves him and kisses him?" Margaret thought she could detect angst in Ben's eyes as he spoke those words.

"It does seem rather odd to me."

Sophie came and took her hand. "I suffer from depression. I have since I was a child. My parents were very old when I was born. They didn't want me and basically ignored me every chance they got. My father used to tell me he wished I was never born. Then in my teenage years, my cousins... well, let's just say they were not happy times."

She paused and Ben pulled her against his chest. "Because of that, Sophie is fragile."

Sophie continued. "I moved to the UK to get away from my family. Tried to live a normal life. But I discovered a different type of cruelty in the way my so-called friends treated me. Time and again, they set me up as the butt of their jokes. Not one single person cared about me in the slightest. After one particularly humiliating event, I decided I'd had enough." Sophie wiped her cheeks. "I decided to end it all. I had the pills all counted out. Booze to give me courage chilled in the fridge. I'd even written my suicide note. I planned to do myself in that night, after I tied up my last loose ends at work." She sobbed.

Margaret noted how, despite Ben's arms holding Sophie's body, the woman reached for Henry's hand and clung tightly to it.

"That last morning was the day I met your brother. And those evil witches wasted no time in telling Henry all my faults and mistakes. Do you know what your brother did?"

Margaret looked around the room. Compassion showed in the other three adults' eyes as they watched Sophie. The blonde's eyes were red as she watched Margaret. "No."

"He confronted them and called them out for exactly what they were. Bullies. Henry made it clear he wouldn't tolerate anyone bullying me and furthermore, he announced that anyone who tried would have to answer to him. That was the first time in my life that anyone stood up for me. The greatest act of kindness I'd ever experienced. That night, when I arrived home, I decided to put off the suicide for one day, then another and another until I finally got rid of the pills." She again wiped her eyes. "If not for Henry, I wouldn't be here. So, when you hear me tell your brother I love him so much, it's because he saved my life."

It was hard to swallow the lump in her throat. "I, uh, I didn't know."

Ellie's voice was soft. "Sophie and I have both suffered from severe bouts of depression. If not for my Aunt Katie and Uncle Jeremy intervening, the alcoholism I turned to might have claimed my life. It goes into remission, but depression is cruel. It never really seems to go away. It's always right there under the surface and lurking on the edge of your mind."

Henry released Sophie's hand and then stood next to Ellie, arm around his wife.

She smiled. "Friendship, deep, deep friendship and love is what gets us through. And if what Sophie needs is that friendship and love, I'm fine with that."

The corner of her eye caught Ben's movement. He gently kissed Sophie's head. "And I'm totally okay with it, too."

Sophie turned and kissed her husband. "God blessed me with such an awesome husband. I love you, Benjy."

Ellie reached for Margaret's hand, but spoke to Henry. "I think it's time to introduce Margaret to her nephew. Would you mind retrieving our son?"

"I'd like to meet him."

Ellie pulled her close. "Deep friendship. The type you and I used to, and still have. That's the true secret of life."

Hours later, after a long and happy visit with her family, Margaret walked to her Land Rover. Ellie's words echoed through her heart and mind. *Deep friendship—the true secret of life.* Exactly what she and Joe shared. *I can't wait to see you and kiss your lips for the first time.* It was funny how a morning that started so poorly turned into a great day. And that would get better when he got home. *How soon until you get home, Joe?*

# Chapter Twenty-one

*Early Monday Morning in Pennsylvania,*
*Mid-afternoon in the Philippines*

Joe concentrated to hear the youth's heartbeat against the sound of the wind as it tore through the flaps of the tent. The morning briefing had predicted another major storm, but this weather was hours in front of the prediction. The Marine master sergeant in charge of the security escort walked into the enclosure where Joe and his assistant, Navy corpsman Baker, were seeing patients.

The leatherneck yelled to be heard over the weather, "Doc, I just got word from command. We're pulling the plug on today's mission. Conditions are deteriorating. The carrier group is in route to reposition away from the storm, so it's going to be a longer flight out than it was to get here this morning. Finish with this patient, then help tear down."

Joe glanced out of the flap at the crowd of people still waiting to be seen. "What about them? There's women and children out there who need our help."

"Sorry, doc. My priorities are to protect U.S. personnel... American lives... first. We need to get moving, now. Our ride will be here in fifteen minutes. Now, if you'll excuse me, I'm going to secure the LZ."

Joe turned to the corpsman. "But those people need our assistance."

The man shook his head. "Sir, orders are orders. I don't like how the wind has picked up. I'm not looking forward to a dicey ride back in the helo." The sailor began collecting their supplies and storing them in the containers. Within ten minutes, you couldn't even tell that there had been an evaluation site at this location.

Much to his surprise, Joe looked up to see a convoy of four helicopters approaching. With the noise of the wind, he hadn't even heard their approach. With military precision, all the supplies and personnel were swiftly loaded. From his vantage point strapped inside the airframe, Joe saw the crowd surge toward the airships. Though he couldn't hear it, Joe could see the flame coming from the master sergeant's rifle as he pointed it and fired skyward. Like magic, the crowd froze, then turned as one and finally dissipated like a wisp of vapor. After the other three ships had rotated into the sky, Joe noted how the Marines climbed onto the last bird, their gritty old commander the last one to step aboard.

This ride was nothing like he'd ever experienced. The metal ship was tossed side to side in addition to up and down. When they crossed over the shoreline, Joe's eyes were glued to the ferocity of the waves pounding the sand. "Those waves must be twenty or thirty feet high."

Baker replied in the headset. "Do you surf, doc? You'd get some real action on those."

Joe hadn't realized he'd spoken out loud. "I don't think so."

The flight surgeon in charge of the medical detail laughed as everyone was thrown around yet again. She quipped, "What's wrong, Dr. Rohrer? Does a little bit of turbulence bother you? Does it make your tummy queasy?" She handed him a plastic bag.

There was laughter on the headset until a heavy jarring motion reverberated through the ship. Judging by the concerned looks on the faces of the team, something wasn't right. Additional bangs and clunks shook the chopper.

A calm female voice filled his ears, despite the background sound of warning indicators. "Everyone, hold on. We are experiencing what appears to be a mechanical failure. I've requested and received clearance to land on the nearest ship, the Anzio. She's about thirty clicks out, so this will be one wild ride. And maybe a wet one. Don your life vests and remain in your restraints. That's an order."

The next fifteen minutes were chaotic. The vibration and bouncing of the ship in unstable air made every sense, including Joe's vision, almost impossible to interpret. The airframe calmed for a second and Joe caught a glimpse of a ship. He guessed by its size it was a cruiser, but it was being tossed about in the wild sea as if it were a leaf in a tornado. The helipad on the stern was illuminated.

Joe hadn't realized how dark the sky had become until he noticed the brightness of the lights along the rim of the helipad.

The pilot was obviously highly skilled as she guided the vehicle over the rolling deck. Joe guessed they were hovering twenty feet off the pad. But when the pilot made her move to drop the helicopter onto a firm foundation, the wind shoved them sideways. The chopper started to roll to his left. The sound of metal striking metal filled his ears.

As if in slow motion, the helicopter tipped over the side of the warship. Every loose item inside the cabin rocketed, bouncing first against the door to Joe's left, then ending up on the ceiling. Harsh drumbeat-like noise eclipsed the storm's fury as the helicopter's rotor beat against the ship's hull.

Within seconds, sparks of metal fragments peppered the helicopter's bulkhead and windshield. Suddenly the glass exploded and large chunks of flying metal slammed into Joe's body. Amid excruciating pain, he noted water filling the cabin. The rising liquid had already covered Joe's nose and mouth when his sight failed and everything went dark.

***

Leslie walked into the showroom. It was Thursday morning. Rebecca was helping the new girl set up a display. When the Amish girl noted Leslie was there, her face broke into a wide smile. Rebecca excused herself and came over to share a brief hug.

"Hey, Becky. How are you today?"

It didn't seem anyone could possibly miss the stars in her friend's eyes. "I've never been better. And how are you this fine morning?" Leslie knew the reason for Rebecca's happiness. It was because of a man named Golden... not Leslie's husband Isaac, but Isaac's twin, Abraham.

"I'm well. Have you seen Maggie?"

Rebecca's smile transformed into a frown. "I believe she's in her office. I'm really concerned about her. She didn't look so gud when she came in."

"What do you think is wrong?"

"I believe it has something to do with Dr. Rohrer. On Monday, she was so happy. Maggie told me that she and Joe had made everything right, but her happiness has really gone downhill since. Maybe you should talk to her. I tried but she seems to have shut me out."

Leslie drew a ragged breath. Despite having doubts about Joe's decisions and actions, she couldn't believe he would intentionally go out of his way to hurt Maggie. "I'll try. Will you be joining us again for dinner?"

The smile on the Amish girl's face was back and she raised her eyebrows in anticipation. "Well, Abe did ask me to come over."

"Then I'll see you tonight. Have a great day."

Rebecca turned her attention back to the new employee. Leslie studied the closed door of Maggie's office. After a brief prayer, she knocked.

"Busy. Go away."

Leslie opened the door anyway. Margaret was slumped in her executive chair, gazing at her phone. "I said I'm busy." Her angry expression softened when she looked up. "Sorry Leslie, I didn't know it was you. What can I do for you?"

"I stopped by to talk about tomorrow, but maybe we should discuss what's going on here first."

"I don't know what you mean."

"Come on, girl, we're besties. What's cooking?"

Margaret brushed her cheek. "Joe. I don't understand him. We were so close and then just because we had an argument, he ran away. Doesn't he understand how much I need him, and that he needs me?"

"Speaking from experience, Joe makes some stupid mistakes. But his heart always seemed to be in the right place."

"Did you know he called me on Sunday? We worked through our problems. Joe told me he loved me and I confessed I felt the same way. He encouraged me to make up with my family, which I did. He told me he'd call me Monday morning and we'd talk about when he was coming home... and about our future." The Scottish girl ran her hand through her hair. "Then nothing. I don't understand. What did I do? Was he just playing games with me?"

"That doesn't sound like Joe. Maybe something happened. I saw on the news that the Philippines got hit with another storm. Could that be why he hasn't called?"

"I don't know." Margaret shook her head. "Look, I don't want to talk about it anymore. Can we change the subject?"

Leslie could empathize with the sorrow Margaret was experiencing. Leslie had gone through it herself when she broke up with Joe. Luckily, her family had been there and supported her. That got her through. That and the fact that Isaac had been waiting. "Of course, Maggie, but I'll always be here for you. You know that, don't you?"

"Yes. Now you mentioned tomorrow? What's... oh right. Didi's husband is coming home. I bet she's ecstatic."

"Not really. Didi's pretty worried. She tried to reach out to Luke, but he refused to talk to her. I can't imagine the trauma her husband went through. A prisoner of war for over three years? It's not much, but I want to make sure everything goes well for his homecoming party. Can you help?"

Margaret sighed. "Wouldn't miss it for the world. What time do you want me there?"

"His flight arrives in Philly about nine, so Didi expects they'll get home around noon. Did you see the fuss the local news stations have been making about his homecoming?"

"No, I don't watch the news anymore."

"They're encouraging the public to come out and welcome him. It's going to be a big event. I just hope Luke can handle it. At least for Didi's sake."

"Well, I'm glad Didi's husband is finally returning. I wish Joe was coming home, too."

\*\*\*

The scent of fried chicken filled the kitchen. Despite the homey aroma, Leslie's heart was heavy. Isaac was draining the potatoes, masher in hand.

"Buttercup, what's wrong?"

He knew her so well. "This whole thing with Joe not calling Maggie, letting her down. I don't understand. Why wouldn't he call?"

"Maybe something happened and he can't? Humanitarian missions can be touchy sometimes, especially when there's unrest, like the news has been reporting. I'm no expert on your ex-boyfriend, but I do believe he's a standup kind of guy. There has to be an explanation."

Leslie's hand covered her mouth. "You don't think he was injured, do you?" Isaac shrugged his shoulders. "Wouldn't the military call or something?"

"Who is his next of kin?"

"His sister, Frannie."

Dropping a stick of butter into the steaming pile of potatoes, Isaac started mashing them. "Call her."

"I can't. Remember, I broke up with him."

"Hmm, got her number?"

"Of course."

"I'll call. After all, Maggie is my boss. I don't mind asking. What's the worst she can do? Tell me to go pound sand?"

Leslie chewed on her lip for a second. "Her husband was in the Army. Maybe that would work. She might understand if you called."

She found Joe's sister's number in her contacts and gave it to Isaac. Her husband didn't hesitate. She eavesdropped as best as she could. Isaac identified himself and stated the reason for his call. Her heart was in her throat when his face paled.

"A helicopter crash? How serious? Good Lord. I'm so sorry. When are they bringing him home? Tomorrow? I understand. Yes, it's not my story to tell, so I'll keep it to myself. Our condolences are with you and your family. Thank you for your time and we'll keep all of you in our prayers. Goodbye."

Leslie's hands were shaking when she touched Isaac's arm. "Wh-what did she say?"

Isaac's face was filled with compassion. *Oh God. Bad news.* Isaac pulled over a kitchen stool. "Leslie, I think you need to sit down."

## Chapter Twenty-two

*Friday Morning*

argaret was confused about the way Leslie was acting. Her friend's ever-present smile was missing. Margaret could have sworn Leslie sobbed when they embraced. Despite Margaret's questions, Leslie only wanted to discuss the preparations. A line of people waiting to greet Luke snaked off into the distance as far as the eye could see.

The food for the event had been donated by local businesses. Hannah and Sam Espenshade had brought along a tub of oatmeal whoopee pies—Luke and Didi's favorites, according to Hannah—as well as two dozen sheet cakes. Mountains of sandwiches, trays of veggies and coolers full of drinks filled the tables on the lawn.

Margaret was puzzled as she checked out what appeared to be a wedding cake. A bride and groom decoration topped the uppermost layer, along with the figurine of a small boy, but "Welcome Home Luke" was written on the foundation.

"Seems strange, having a wedding cake today, doesn't it?"

Margaret turned to find Hannah standing there. "Yes. Is there a story behind it?"

Hannah's smile was dazzling. "Luke and Didi got married the day before he shipped out. He promised her a big wedding when he returned. Didi asked me to make it, as a joke. You see, they only spent one night together and their son LBJ was the result." Hannah sighed. "Those two had the same wacky sense of humor. I hope Luke retained his."

Honking horns signaled in the distance. Leslie was suddenly there. "It looks like the procession is coming." Two state police cruisers pulled up in front of the house, lights flashing. A long limousine was next. A military band started playing "America the Beautiful" as the door to the limo swung open. A woman Leslie identified as Luke's mother lunged inside. Luke's own brothers, clothed in their United States Marine Corps dress blues helped their brother out of the vehicle. A roar rose up from everyone.

Luke steadied himself on two canes, and then reached for his wife's hand. The poor man's face was gaunt and his body deathly thin. Didi's cheeks were soaked, but Margaret had never seen Didi's smile be as wide as it was. Together the couple moved to a pair of beautifully decorated chairs in front of the house. In disbelief, Margaret watched as one by one, the line of people greeted Luke and Didi with a hug or a kiss. The promenade continued for hours.

Recognizing a special group of people, Margaret ran over to greet them all with hugs. Henry welcomed her with outstretched arms, as did Sophie and Ellie.

Ellie was in a wheelchair and squeezed Margaret extra tight. "I love you, sis."

While waiting for the line to dwindle, Margaret socialized with her family.

Finally, the crowd was down to almost nothing. Hannah, Sam, Leslie and Margaret were the last four to welcome the hero home.

Didi embraced each in turn. Despite the look of exhaustion, Margaret knew Didi was overjoyed. She spoke to Luke, but her eyes were on the quartet. "Luke, these are *our* closest friends. They made sure I stayed sane by constantly building me up with words of hope and love. They're friends that have become family, so we're going to have frequent get togethers."

Luke gave out an exhausted laugh. "Once Didi and I get reacquainted, we'll have a party." He winked at his wife. "Haven't had one of those in a long while. G'night, everyone."

Leslie wrapped her arm through Margaret's as they walked to their vehicles. Leslie's voice was shaky. "What an emotional day. I'm so glad they're back together. We should do this again."

"Do what?"

"Oh, have parties, you know?"

Margaret gave her a strange look. "When were you thinking?"

Leslie quickly dabbed her eyes. "Soon, Maggie, soon. The world needs more celebrations." Leslie's mouth opened, but shut just as quickly. "Good night, Maggie." Leslie again hugged her, very tightly.

"Night."

On the ride home, Joe was on the forefront of Maggie's mind. *Are you coming home? Or have I seen the last of you?*

Margaret was exhausted. She was exceptionally glad when the driveway appeared in her headlights. But getting out of the Land Rover, she noticed something was amiss. The living room lights were shining through the curtains. Despite the tendrils of fear climbing her spine, she approached the front door. Before she could insert the key in the lock, the door swung open. Instinctively, Margaret shifted to a defensive position, house key gripped tightly and ready to be used, if need be.

But she quickly recognized the face of the woman standing there. It was Joe's friend, Daisy. There was a man with her. *Who is he?* "Daisy. You startled me. What are you doing here?"

A smile covered the other woman's face. "This is my husband, Jake. Jake, this is Margaret, Joe's girl."

*Joe's girl?* Had she heard correctly?

The man extended his hand. "Pleased to meet you. Now, if you'll excuse us, it's been a very long day."

"Uh, okay. Wait, why are you here?"

Margaret caught the secretive look between them. Daisy answered. "We were just checking on something. I don't mean to be rude, but it has been quite a day. By the way, we saw you on the news."

"News? What are you talking about?"

The man now spoke. "The Harrisburg station had coverage of Luke Zinn's homecoming. We saw you in some of the background shots."

"Oh, I didn't know. It was a long day for me as well." Margaret's nose tingled. "I kept wishing it was Joe who was coming home."

Daisy giggled, which Margaret thought was odd. "Joe Rohrer wouldn't want all the fanfare. He's a private kind of guy. But I guess you know that better than anyone." The woman again glanced at her husband. Though she couldn't read it, Margaret knew there was some unspoken communication going on. The brunette returned her attention to Margaret. "We must be going, but we'll see you again... real, real soon."

And just like that, the pair left. Margaret stood watching them as they climbed into a white Fusion parked along the street. She hadn't even seen it sitting there. After waving goodbye, she entered the house and then paused. A strange scent she couldn't immediately identify greeted her. After a few seconds, it came to her. It was the sterile kind of odor one noted in a hospital. Margaret walked through the kitchen toward the living room. The scent grew stronger. The hair on the back of her neck stood on end when she realized someone was sitting on the love seat.

"Hi, Maggie. I missed you, Welcome home."

"Joe?" She barely recognized the man. The top of his head was wrapped in gauze. Five bandages were evident on his face. His left leg was in a cast. But her eyes drifted back to his heavily wrapped left arm, which ended just below the elbow. "Is this really you?"

He nodded and held his good arm open for her. Margaret knelt before him and held him tightly. "I missed you so much. Don't you ever leave me like that again."

He kissed the side of her head. To her surprise his body convulsed and a sob escaped from his lips.

"What's wrong?"

"I was so afraid... afraid I'd never see you again. I thought I was dead."

Maggie grazed his cheek with her lips. "Shh. It's okay. I'm right here."

He drew her in tighter, whispering in her ear. "I promise, I'll never leave you again." He sniffed hard. "Look at me, Maggie."

She pulled back. His image was wavy before her eyes. Joe's face was filled with something she'd never noticed before.

With his right hand, he touched her face. "I love you, Maggie. I need you." Joe wiped his cheeks and then giggled. Holding up the stump of his arm, he smiled. "I plan on staying by your side, because, you see, I tend to fall apart when you're not around."

It was her turn to laugh and dry her eyes. "Just like you to make a joke at a time like this."

Joe drew her tight again. "I never want us to end. This may seem sudden to you, but I've been ready to ask this for a while. Will you marry me, Maggie? I know I need to get the ring and ask your brother Henry for permission and all that stuff, but I really want to spend the rest of my life with you, not just as my best friend, but as my wife. I love you."

It was hard to catch her breath. The shock of seeing him again, understanding his injuries and now a proposal? "But we haven't even had our first kiss yet."

"Then let's remedy that right now." Joe's lips found hers and for the first time in her life, everything was right, no, perfect. His lips slowly started to move away, but Margaret pulled his head back for more. The softness of that kiss eclipsed the first.

*This is heaven.* "Ask me again."

His smile and those eyes, oh how they made her feel giddy. "Will you marry me, Maggie?"

"Just so you know, I may not have expressed it out loud, but I've been in love with you for years. You asking that question has been my dream since the first time we met. And the answer has been on my lips, waiting for a chance for me to say it. So, Joseph Rohrer, the answer is yes. I'd be honored to be your wife."

The next kiss carried them away.

# Epilogue

*December*

Joe was back in the chopper as it hovered in the storm. Rocking violently in the massive waves, the ship waited twenty feet below. But when the pilot dropped the Sikorsky Sea Hawk to the deck, a gust of wind shoved the eight-ton airship to the port railing before tipping it over the side of the ship.

A metal container struck Joe in the jaw before bouncing to the ceiling. The pounding noise of the rotors striking against the hull was deafening. In disbelief, he was a spectator to the whirring chunk of rotor blade that ripped through the door and sliced through his arm. Additional metal fragments penetrated the helicopter's door, some peppering his skin with a searing heat.

The intensity of the pain was too much to take and he lost consciousness. And then, he was sinking beneath the water in the darkness. Suddenly, the sound of her voice beckoned to him. Joe reached for the angel above him, but the aircraft lurched. He knew it was dropping to the bottom of the Pacific

233

Ocean... and taking his life with it. In frustration, Joe franticly swam toward the vision of Maggie while screaming her name.

The warmth of her embrace penetrated the chill in his body. She was holding him, not in his dream, but in real life. "Shh, Joey. It's just a bad dream. You're safe now. I love you and I'll protect you from anything, forever and always. It's okay, babe."

The trembling gradually slowed down, thanks to the love of his wife. Her lips touched his face and neck as she chased away the night terrors.

"Want to talk about it?"

"It was pretty much the same nightmare as before. I was drowning." He raised his eyes to meet hers. "And just like when it really happened, it was you. You saved me. You called to me and I followed the sound of your voice. I think God sends those dreams to remind me how much I need you. I have all along, you know. You're my angel, Maggie Rohrer. I love you."

"I love you, too." She kissed him. "Let me hold you until you fall asleep."

In her arms, Joe drifted off to slumber and his dreams began again. But this time, instead of a nightmare, peaceful pleasant images walked his mind as the angel of his dreams held him tightly.

\*\*\*

Margaret squeezed Joe's right hand as they stood in line, ready to disembark. She couldn't help but smile as she felt their wedding rings touch—hers on her left hand and his on his right. "Puerta Vallarta. Can you believe it was just one short year ago that we ran into each other down here? And look at us now... you tricked me into marrying you."

He grunted, but she couldn't miss the joy in his eyes. "Who tricked who? It seems I offered to let you buy my house at a very cheap price, but instead... you used matrimony to save your money and become half owner, without losing a cent."

*Joe does love to play, doesn't he?* "I don't know. You made out all right, ending up half owner in a vineyard you didn't plant. Talk about stealing wealth... you gold digger."

Joe spun her toward him, his lips eager to find hers. His warmth and the taste of his lips ignited desire deep within her. Margaret couldn't help it. She threw her arms around him and kissed him with a fiery intensity.

"Well, well. If it isn't our newlyweds. Will you be going ashore or spending the day, uh, celebrating in your stateroom?"

Releasing each other, they both turned to see the identity of the man. His face cracked wide with a smile. It was their dining room server, who apparently had been unfortunate enough to draw disembarkation station duty this morning.

Joe cleared his throat and answered, "My bride and I will be going into town, thank you. You know, it was at this same port last year that we met, right in a little cantina down the street. And we had such a wonderful time."

"Is that when you two fell in love?"

Eyeing the man still holding her hand, the memories came back. Not only of that day, but the day she'd first met him. She twittered and then replied, "I fell in love with Joe a long time ago, but seeing him again, here, reminded me of my dreams and how much I hoped and prayed someday we'd be together."

Her husband's mouth dropped open and he stared at her in astonishment. "A long time ago? When?"

He was so handsome, despite the scars. She touched his face. "You were with Tara, right after she and Edmund had that fight. The two of you were shopping, at Roots. I saw you and knew... right then... you were the only man for me." She pulled him in for another kiss.

"Such a nice story, but there's a big line behind you. If you're not heading back to your room, I'd suggest you step forward." The man reviewed their passports and then scanned their access cards. "Have a nice day. Oh, I forgot to tell you, if you take any taxis, only use the ones here at the terminal."

The married couple shared a knowing look and giggled. But even before they stepped on the dock, she sensed something was on his mind. "What's going on, Joey?"

His laughter surprised her. "I was just remembering last year, when I looked up and saw your pretty face. Never would have imagined I'd just met the woman of my dreams. It's been quite a journey, hasn't it?"

"A good one, I hope."

He held up the stump of his left arm. "There's one thing I do regret."

Sorrow cast a shadow on their walk. "Losing your arm?"

Joe wrapped his good arm around her tightly. "No, well yes, I do regret that, but I was thinking about how I ran out on you. I was selfish, only caring about myself and my feelings. I abandoned my best friend."

She rested her head on his shoulder as they walked. "Sometimes you need to go through the bad times to appreciate the good ones. If things hadn't gone as they did, do you believe we would have gotten married on Thanksgiving?"

His lips gently touched the top of her head. "No, and once again I find you're right. Maggie, you are the most intelligent woman I've ever met. And the most beautiful, and romantic, and thoughtful and... I could go on and on." His words sobered. "If the loss of a limb was the price of winning your heart, I got a real deal. And as long as I have one arm to hold you tight, I'm happy. I'm so in love with you, Maggie. I hope you know how much."

She giggled. "Why don't you tell me?"

The smile on his lips made her heart race. "Hmm, I love you enough to have allowed you to choose my last ex-girlfriend to be your maid of honor. I think that's proof enough."

*So, you want to tease, eh?* "At least I didn't have a man serve as my maid of honor. I still am puzzled that you chose a woman to serve as your best man. Is there something I need to worry about? And what did you call Daisy... best woman?"

"There is and never will be anything to worry about. No, the official title was best person. I married the best woman."

"Nice recovery." Margaret caught a glimpse of a girl with a familiar face. She lowered her voice. "Joe, see that girl over there?"

"Sweetheart, we're newlyweds, I don't want to look at any other woman."

"Thanks, but see her? The one with the white t-shirt?"

He glanced at the youth. "Okay. So?"

A giggle slipped out. "That's the pickpocket I told you about. I walked in the bar to get away from her last year and that's when I ran into you."

Joe alternated his view between Margaret and the pickpocket. His hand fumbled in his right front pants pocket for a second. "Be right back, Maggie."

"Where are you going?"

But he was already gone, walking until he stood in front of the thief. He held something in his hand. The girl took it and ran off down the street. Smiling, her husband returned.

Margaret was curious. "What was that about?"

Joe's arm pulled her in and his lips found hers. "I gave her a tip, for sending you into that bar to get my attention."

Her fingers touched his cheek. "I should have been the one who rewarded her. You see, I'm the one who got the real prize." Their lips met again. "I love you, Joey."

"And I love you, Maggie."

Hand in hand they strolled through the tourist resort. She almost jumped when he spoke. "I'm not sure I want to return to the medical field."

"Why not?"

He sighed and his eyes carried a far-off look. "I feel like I have achieved my goal of helping people. I've entered a different phase of my life... now."

"And what chapter are you in?"

He stopped and she faced him. "My favorite one... the one where I get to spend every single second of every day by your side. I have to pinch myself sometimes to make sure this isn't only a dream. Let's face it, how could a man as simple as me ever get lucky enough to marry you, let alone have you as my best friend? I haven't had a lot of luck with romance... until you."

"I'll let you in on a secret. Ever since that first day I saw you, I had a feeling you were the one for me. Even as you bounced from girl to girl, I couldn't get that thought out of my head. I wanted us to end up together."

"And I was too dumb to realize that. I almost squandered the best thing to ever happen to me. Suppose I wouldn't have decided to return home? I was planning on staying in Hawaii, you know."

"That's simple. I would have followed you."

"But your vineyard, your dream was your winery in Paradise."

Margaret made sure he was looking in her eyes. "The vineyard is only a thing, a possession. The real dream was for us to wind up together, forever." Margaret kissed her husband. "I hope you know by now... For me... Paradise will always be wherever you are."

The End

# Enjoyed this book?
Please consider placing a review on Amazon!
This will help other readers find great books.

*Get exclusive*
*never-before-published content!*

www.chaswilliamson.com

*A Paradise Short Story*

Download your free copy of
*Skating in Paradise* today!

# Other Books by this Author

**Seeking Forever (Book 1)**
Kaitlin Jenkins long ago gave up the notion of ever finding true love, let alone a soulmate. Jeremy is trying to get his life back on track after a bitter divorce and an earlier than planned departure from the military. They have nothing in common, except their distrust of the opposite sex.

An unexpected turn of events sends these two strangers together on a cross-country journey—a trip fraught with loneliness and unexpected danger. And on this strange voyage, they're forced to rely on each other—if they want to survive. But after the past, is it even possible to trust anyone again?

*Seeking Forever* is the first book of Chas Williamson's Seeking series, the saga of the Jenkins family over three generations.

Will Kaitlin and Jeremy ever be the same after this treacherous journey?

## Seeking Happiness (Book 2)

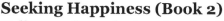

Kelly was floored when her husband of ten years announced he was leaving her for another woman. But she isn't ready to be an old maid. And she soon discovers there's no shortage of men waiting in line.

Every man has his flaws, but sometimes the most glaring ones are well hidden. And now and then, those faults can force other people to the very edge, to become everything they're not. And when that happens to her, there's only one thing that can save Kelly.

*Seeking Happiness* is the second book of Chas Williamson's Seeking series, the saga of the Jenkins family over three generations.

Ride along with Kelly on one of the wildest adventures you can imagine.

## Seeking Eternity (Book 3)

At eighteen, Nora Thomas fell in love with her soulmate and best friend, Stan Jenkins. But Nora was already engaged to a wonderful man, so reluctantly, Nora told Stan they could only be friends. Stan completely disappeared (well, almost), from her world, from her life, from everywhere but Nora's broken heart.

Ten painful years later, the widow and mother of two was waiting tables when she looked up and found

Stan sitting in her section. But she was wearing an engagement ring and Stan, a wedding ring. Can a woman survive when her heart is ripped out a second time?

*Seeking Eternity* is the third book of Chas Williamson's Seeking series, a glimpse at the beginning of the Jenkins' family saga through three generations.

Will Nora overcome all odds to find eternal happiness?

### Seeking the Pearl (Book 4)

Eleanor Lucia has lived a sad and somber life, until she travels to London to open a hotel for her Aunt Kaitlin. For that's where Ellie meets Scotsman Henry Campbell and finally discovers true happiness. All that changes when Ellie disappears without a trace and everyone believes she is dead, well almost everyone.

But Henry and Ellie have a special bond, one that defies explanation. As if she were whispering in his ear, Henry can sense Eleanor begging him to save her. And Henry vows he will search for her, he will find her and he will rescue her, or spend his last breath trying.

*Seeking the Pearl* is the exciting finale of Chas Williamson's Seeking series, the culmination of the three generation Jenkins' family saga.

Henry frantically races against time to rescue Ellie, but will he be too late?

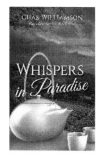

### Whispers in Paradise (Book 1)

Ashley never expected to find love, not after what cancer had done to her body. Until Harry Campbell courts her in a fairy tale romance that exceeds even her wildest dreams. But all that changes in an instant when Harry's youngest brother steals a kiss, and Harry walks in on it.

Just when all her hopes and dreams are within reach, Ashley's world crumbles. Life is too painful to remain in Paradise because Harry's memory taunts her constantly. Yet for a woman who has beaten the odds, defeating cancer not once, but twice, can anything stand in the way of her dreams?

*Whispers in Paradise* is the first book in Chas Williamson's Paradise series, stories based loosely around the loves and lives of the patrons of Sophie Miller's Essence of Tuscany Tea Room.

Which brother will Ashley choose?

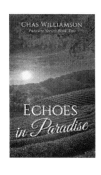

### Echoes in Paradise (Book 2)

Hannah Rutledge rips her daughters from their Oklahoma home in the middle of the night to escape a predator from her youth. After months of secrecy and frequent moves to hide her trail, she settles in

Paradise and ends up working with Sam Espenshade, twelve years her junior. Sam wins her daughters' hearts, and earns her friendship, but because of her past, can she ever totally trust anyone again?

Yet, for the first time since the death of her husband, Hannah's life is starting to feel normal, and happy, very happy. But a violent attack leaves Sam physically scarred and drives a deep wedge between them. To help heal the wounds, Hannah is forced from her comfort zone and possibly exposes the trail she's tried so hard to cover.

*Echoes in Paradise* is the second book in Chas Williamson's Paradise series, an exciting love story with Sophie Miller's Essence of Tuscany Tea Room in background.

When the villain's brother shows up on Hannah's doorstep at midnight on Christmas night, were the efforts since she left Oklahoma in vain?

### Courage in Paradise (Book 3)

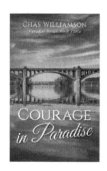

Sportscaster Riley Espenshade returns to southcentral Pennsylvania so she can be close to her family while growing her career. One thing Riley didn't anticipate was falling for hockey's greatest superstar, Mickey Campeau, a rough and tall Canadian who always gets what he wants... and that happens to be Riley. Total bliss seems to be at her fingertips, until she discovers Mickey also loves another girl.

The "other girl" happens to be Molly, a two-year old orphan suffering from a very rare childhood cancer. Meanwhile, Riley's shining career is rising to its zenith when a new sports network interviews her to be the lead anchor. Just when her dream job falls into her lap, Mickey springs his plan on her—a quick marriage, adopting Molly and setting up house.

*Courage in Paradise* is Chas Williamson's third book in the Paradise series, chronicling the loves and lives of those who frequent Sophie Miller's Essence of Tuscany Tea Room.

Riley is forced to make a decision, but which one will she choose?

### Stranded in Paradise (Book 4)

When Aubrey Stettinger is attacked on a train, a tall, handsome stranger comes to her assistance, but disappears just as quickly. Four months later, Aubrey finds herself recuperating in Paradise at the home of a friend of a friend.

When she realizes the host's brother is the hero from the train, she suspects their reunion is more than a coincidence. Slowly, and for the first time in her life, Aubrey begins to trust—in family, in God and in a man. But just when she's ready to let her guard down, life once again reminds her she can't trust anyone. Caught between two worlds, Aubrey must choose between chasing her fleeting dreams and carving out a new life in this strange place.

*Stranded in Paradise* is the fourth book in the Paradise series, chronicling the loves and lives of those who frequent Sophie Miller's Essence of Tuscany Tea Room.

Will Aubrey remain *Stranded in Paradise*?

### Christmas in Paradise (Book 5)

True love never dies, except when it abandons you at the altar.

Rachel Domitar has found the man of her dreams. The church is filled with friends and family, her hair and dress are perfect, and the honeymoon beckons, but one knock at the door is about to change everything.

Leslie Lapp's life is idyllic—she owns her own business and home, and has many friends—but no one special to share her life... until one dark and stormy afternoon when she's forced off the highway. Will the knock at her door be life changing as well?

When love comes knocking at Christmas, will they have the courage to open the door to paradise?

# About the Author

Chas Williamson's lifelong dream was to write. He started writing his first book at age eight, but quit after two paragraphs. Yet some dreams never fade...

It's said one should write what one knows best. That left two choices—the world of environmental health and safety... or romance. Chas and his bride have built a fairytale life of love. At her encouragement, he began writing romance. The characters you'll meet in his books are very real to him, and he hopes they'll become just as real to you.

True Love Lasts Forever!

*Follow Chas on*
*www.bookbub.com/authors/chas-williamson*

Made in the USA
Middletown, DE
16 September 2021